Falling for the Football Player

Clearview Falls University
Book 3

S.E. Rose

Sierra Hill

Note to Readers:
*This book includes reference to mental health issues and
past trauma. Some readers may have sensitivity to these
subjects.*

Prologue

elsie - December in Paris

> Me: Hey, baby, are you on your way?

> Me: I'm waiting for you at our spot in front of La Sacré-Cœur. In case you forgot where we said we'd meet.

> Me: Where are you? It's getting cold and late.

> Me: Are you okay???

The texts on my phone have become more urgent over the past fifteen minutes while I'm sitting on the steps in front of the famous Montmartre cathedral. I've been waiting for Hayes to meet me here like we planned and discussed yesterday.

The longer I've been out in the cold and dark—and the fact that he hasn't responded to any of my texts—has made me very grumpy and more than a little pissed at him right now.

I lift my head and glance around at all the people milling about, checking to see if he's anywhere to be found, and recall our conversation from just last night while lying in bed together.

"Do you mind if we stop at the Christmas market before we go to Aunt Desiree's?" I'd asked, sliding my fingers through his long, wavy hair. Falling in soft waves over his shoulders, it was the first thing I noticed about him the day we met. "I want to pick up some flowers and wine to bring with us."

We agreed that we'd meet here at 4 p.m. today before stopping by the market. From there, we'd head to my aunt's place a block from the market for Christmas Eve dinner and our gift exchange.

But Hayes is nowhere to be seen.

Where the hell is he?

My mind goes through a number of scenarios and reasons why he hasn't shown up yet. Maybe he got sick and is lying in bed with a fever?

Or was he mugged on the way here and left for dead?

Neither of these horrible possibilities makes me feel any better as I pace around at the bottom of the steps pondering the only other alternative.

That Hayes would stand me up on Christmas Eve.

I can't even fathom that one because why would he do that when just the other night he told me he loved me?

We'd just finished dinner and wine, and we were enjoying a walk along the banks of the Seine River. The moon glittered off the water as the twinkling lights from the

Eiffel Tower gleamed like diamonds before us as we strolled hand in hand and stopped over the bridge to enjoy the view. That's when he turned to me, framed my face in his hands, and said, "*Mon amour, je t'aime. Tu es si belle. I'm so lucky to have met you.*"

He was always telling me how beautiful I am, but this was the first time he said he loves me. Then he kissed me so thoroughly, my toes curled inside my shoes from the sheer pleasure of his touch.

I didn't return the sentiment but I know I feel it too. Meeting Hayes here in Paris was like fate. What I feel for him is something I've never felt before.

The funny thing is that Hayes was only meant to be a fun and quick fling.

When I saw him sitting alone outside that Paris café the day before my classes started, I couldn't resist asking him out. I'd half expected that we'd spend the day together checking out the touristy sites, have some dinner and drinks, and then go back to my place to fuck. Then, *voilá*, he'd be on his way and I'd never see him again.

That was four months ago and all the days I've spent with him have been the best days of my life. As luck would have it, he is a U.S. student also studying abroad in the same International Business program as me.

See? It was fate.

Just yesterday, over a video call with my best friends Grace and Lucy, I spilled the tea and told them about Hayes and how I think I'm in love. They were both shocked over my revelation, but excited for my newfound relationship. The three of us laughed just like old times and made plans for when I return to school in January.

Grumbling now over not wanting to waste any more precious time, I brush off the wet snow that's begun to fall and has accumulated on the lapels of my peacoat with a sigh. I check my phone one more time on the off chance he's responded to my texts. Then I consider another possibility for his absence. Maybe he got confused and thought he was meeting me at my Auntie D's flat and he's already there having a Christmas drink.

I dial her number, the frustration that's been brewing now turning into something like worry because this is so unlike Hayes.

My aunt picks up on the second ring. I can envision her now, a frothy drink in hand, wearing some gorgeous hand-made necklace around her neck as she floats around the old wooden floors of her apartment.

"*Allo?*"

"DD, it's me. Is Hayes there?" My words come out in a rush.

There's a pause and then she clicks her tongue. "No, not here. Only Alfie and me for now until others arrive," she says, referring to her tiny mutt who looks more like a rat than a dog. "I thought you and Hayes were coming together?"

I do a quick scan of my surroundings, tugging at the scarf I bought earlier this week at the Marché de Noël des Abbesses Christmas market. The breeze has picked up bringing a cold shiver down my back.

Or it could be from the dread that's suddenly infiltrated my mind as I wonder where the hell Hayes is at.

"Yeah, we were...that was the plan. But he hasn't shown up yet. Maybe I should run to his dorm and check on him." I say this more to myself than my aunt. "I'm sorry for the delay. You don't have to wait on us."

"*Oui, d'accord.* I'll ply everyone with drinks and we'll sing songs while we wait. It'll be grand."

This thought makes me giggle, even though I'm not feeling very festive at the moment. My aunt is a famous artist and has loads of friends in Paris. Tonight was supposed to be an intimate holiday dinner with just the three of us and a few of her close friends.

"*Au revoir*. Be there soon."

I hang up and press a hand into my belly, now more than a little fucking worried that something awful has happened to him. Since we met this past summer, Hayes has never once been late and is always good about replying to my messages.

I know something's wrong.

The panic rises in my throat and I swallow it down like a bitter pill as I turn down the street, ready to head in the direction of Hayes's dormitory where he's lived this semester.

Just as I pass the Carrousel de Saint-Pierre on my way toward the Square Louise Michel, my phone chimes with an incoming message.

"Thank God," I mutter, lifting the phone in my hand to read the text.

My feet stall and my head spins like I was just shaken in a snow globe when I read the message he sent.

Hayes: I'm sorry, Kels. I'm not coming.

I'm about to call him to see if he's sick or something. If so, I can bring him some meds and soup and hot tea.

But then his final text squashes those sentiments in a heartbeat.

Hayes: I'm not in Paris anymore. I left this morning. I'm going home. I'm sorry.

Hayes: Goodbye, Kels.

My breath shudders and I clutch at my chest. Is that the sound of icicles falling to the ground and breaking?

No.

It's just my heart shattering into a million little pieces and being scattered and strewn across the Square at the base of the Fontaine des innocents.

My first love has left me and broken my heart.

Now I'll return home to the U.S. having learned an invaluable–if not, difficult—lesson.

I will never love or trust another guy ever again.

Chapter One

K elsie

"I'm back, bitches!" I announce as I enter the house and throw my hands up in the air dramatically. "And tonight I'm going to kiss me a hot guy."

It's my battle cry of sorts because I'm ready to dust myself off and get back on that horse. Taking my two besties by surprise, Lucy and Grace jump from their spots in the living room and squeal with excitement as they rush over to me with wide eyes and outstretched arms.

"Oh, my God, Kelsie! You're home!" Lucy exclaims, her words somewhat muffled against the faux fur lining of the purple coat I brought home from Paris as she embraces me in a tight bear hug. It's the only kind she can give.

Grace joins in on our reunion, but pulls back with a puzzled look across her face. "What are you doing here? I thought you wouldn't be home until Sunday night."

I give them both a cat-that-ate-the-canary smile and shrug off my coat, hanging it in the closet near the front door of the off-campus house we affectionately call the "football house." I can't say I've missed the smell of stale corn chips or the stank of unwashed jerseys from the guys who inhabit the house since I've been gone, but I have sorely missed my two best friends. I could have really used their shoulders to cry on after Hayes dumped me.

Ignoring the painful tug at my heart, I swing my arms around each of their backs and lead them into the room with a phony cheerful tone in my voice.

"There was a slight change in schedules, so I came home early. And, *voilá*, here I am!"

I take a step back and toss my arms out wide, posing in my usual over-the-top *aren't I awesome* manner. My smile is overly bright, even though that light dimmed a few weeks ago.

Both Grace and Lucy know a little about Hayes and the way he ghosted me at Christmas. But I lied about how it broke me into pieces, instead telling them it was what we both wanted in the end. The reality of it was that Hayes and I weren't going to return to the States and continue on a long-distance relationship anyhow. I was prepared for that goodbye, but not the way he delivered it.

Over the last two weeks, I've managed to get through the holidays feeling a myriad of convoluted emotions—the devastation of getting jilted on Christmas Eve and then having to say goodbye to my Aunt Desiree. It's been a lot to handle.

Which is why I made the decision on my long flights home that I was going to hold my head up high, put everything behind me, and start fresh. Fake it til you make it, they say.

And that means I'm going to shove my troubles away and enjoy tonight's festivities.

"Ladies, I am in full party mode tonight and I have only two goals on the agenda." I point my index finger in front of me. "Number one is to celebrate my homecoming with the champagne I brought back from France as a gift to my friends..."

I hook my thumb behind me and both girls turn to see Joel Henderson, or Hendy as everyone calls him, the team quarterback and also house resident, carrying a large box of champagne bottles in his arms. I'd shipped it home because I'd become quite a champagne snob during my time overseas.

Lucy giggles. "Oh, boy, things could get crazy."

"Exactly. And that leads to objective number two, which is to kiss a random guy tonight..." I grin flirtatiously and shimmy my shoulders. "And see where the night leads."

The girls both laugh and Hendy rolls his eyes at my antics as he walks past us through the living room and into the kitchen.

"Is there anyone you haven't kissed on campus yet, Kels?" he lobs out in jest with a flick of his head over his shoulder.

I don't take it as an insult because it's not meant as one. Joel and I go way back to the beginning of our freshman year when he was still a scrawny second-string QB and I was a fun-loving California girl. We had one brief encounter at a dorm party when we made out for a bit, but it didn't go any further than that, or anywhere from there.

As soon as I realized Hendy and I were two peas in a pod, sharing the same opinions on intimacy and relationships, and that my friend Lucy had a secret crush on him, I didn't pursue anything further with him. Now Hendy and I are just good friends who like hanging out with each other and our pals.

I throw out my rebuttal, "Good point...is there anyone *you* haven't kissed, Hendy?"

He laughs, the sound a deep bellow. "*Touché.* But you're looking good tonight, Kels. Paris agreed with you. I'm sure you'll find some sucker to fall at your feet," Hendy compliments, setting the case down on the kitchen table before turning his gaze, roaming it over my body and punctuating it with a chef's kiss.

I give him a polite curtsy and return the appreciative glance with a flirtatious reply. "Why thank you, *monsieur*. You don't look too bad yourself these days."

Now that Lucy has been dating Emmett and has no more feelings toward Hendy, it wouldn't be such a bad thing to hook-up with him if the timing and conditions were right. Although, for the record, I have always tried to avoid football players. With a few exceptions, including Emmett and Grace's boyfriend, Killian, I find football players to be incredibly dull and boring and not at all great lovers. Most of them may have fantastic physiques, but all they do is live, eat, and breathe football. I like a man who's cultured and can hold an intelligent conversation on current affairs or books... and then can talk dirty to me in bed.

Like Hayes.

I shake that thought away and reconsider Hendy. He's changed a lot in the past three years and isn't so bad, except for the way he goes through women. It's a revolving door with him and he's been known to be less than considerate about their feelings.

But what do I expect? He's a guy. And I've learned my lesson when it comes to trusting a man with your heart or your feelings.

"Okay, who's ready to break open some fancy schmancy direct-from-France champagne and get drunk with me?"

Lucy and Grace both raise their hands as Hendy strides off, probably in search of the beer keg.

Grace pulls down some glasses from the cupboard and I pop the champagne cork, pouring the bubbling liquid to the top of each glass, leaving the red Solo cups to the beer guzzlers.

"Let's toast to Kelsie coming home where she belongs!" Grace says, clinking her glass with mine before taking a sip. She hiccups from the fizz and then laughs. "Oh, that's gonna do the trick."

Lucy rubs her nose after her first drink. "It makes my nose tickle."

I lift my glass in the air again and they both do the same.

"Here's to starting a new semester and avoiding all men with stupid first names that should be last names," I say with a little more bitterness than I intend, referring to Hayes, of course. I catch Grace and Lucy eyeing each other.

"I know we're not supposed to mention his name," Grace says hesitantly. "But are you going to tell us the whole story of what happened? One minute you tell us you think you love him and then...poof, it's over." She makes an explosion gesture with her hand.

I down the rest of my glass and refill it, studying the effervescent bubbles as they gather at the top. Then I set the bottle down and wave a hand dismissively.

"Listen, it is what it is and I'm over him," I offer casually, feeling the lie burn inside my throat like battery acid. They can probably see right through me, but neither of them say anything or press further.

The thing is, I've never been dumped by a guy before and it's kind of humiliating, a terrible blow to my ego, as well as my soul. Hayes leaving me like he did punched a big hole in my heart. But I will never admit out loud the pain Hayes caused me. If I can convince my two besties that I'm fine, then I can certainly make myself believe it. "Hayes was nothing more to me than a fling."

Lucy takes a dainty sip of her champagne and raises a disbelieving eyebrow. "But, Kels, didn't you say you loved him?"

Well, shit.

It's not a moment I'm overly proud of. I'd been riding high on that gushy love feeling that you get in your gut and did kind of allude to the idea that I fell for Hayes when I FaceTimed with the girls a few weeks ago. I shake my head adamantly and tilt my head to the side.

"I said *I think* I'm in love," I eagerly correct, hoping to sound more adamant than I feel. "And it doesn't matter anyway because he made his decision when he took off without being man enough to say goodbye to my face. Good riddance, I say. This is exactly why I remain single. All men are cowards and assholes."

"Hey, that's not true," Emmett argues as he strides into the kitchen carrying two grocery bags that look to be filled to the brim with chips and party snacks.

Lucy flicks a look over my shoulder and a huge smile covers her face.

I used to wear that same expression when I saw Hayes in a room.

Swallowing down a huge gulp, I flash a friendly grin at Lucy's boyfriend.

"Hey, EJ. I stand by my statement which is categorically true."

Lucy scoffs and whacks me on the arm with a slap of her hand. I give her a look that says *what?*

"Good to see you too, Kelsie." His eyes are bright as they look from me and then land on Lucy, turning into romantic googly-eyes that make me want to hurl. "Hey, baby. I got you your favorite snack."

She flings her arms around her boyfriend's neck, peppering him with kisses. "*You* are my favorite snack."

I make a gagging noise and spin around. "Oh, God...I need to get out of this love-infested house!"

Grace laughs and latches my wrist in her fingers to keep me in place. "Oh stop it, Kels. I'm sure you saw a ton of kissing and flirtation in Paris. In fact, I bet you got hit on all the time by French men."

"Very true." I flip my hair over my shoulder and offer a flirty smile. "I did appreciate the French way of life. French men know how to demonstrate their affections toward beautiful women."

"There's only one beautiful woman here that I want to french," jumps in Killian, who joins us in the kitchen, lumbering in and grabbing Grace around the waist as she squeals. He picks up her tiny body and pulls her into his gigantic frame where he nuzzles his face into the crook of her neck. Grace lets out a hoot of laughter and I groan again, playfully covering my eyes with my forearm.

"Ewww...*toi aussi*, Gracie?" I lament, dropping my arms from my face and rolling my eyes sarcastically. Killer, the very appropriate nickname for the giant tight end football player, grins and then begins rifling through the grocery bags.

"Did you get me that dip I like, bro?" he asks EJ, quickly refocusing his priorities to food. "I'm starving. And I'm gonna need some major refueling so I can take care of the needs of this sexy girl later tonight."

I sigh. Looks like I've returned to the eye of a love storm and I'm not getting out of it anytime soon.

If I can't beat 'em, I may as well join 'em and have some of my own fun.

"I'm ready to play a game tonight," I announce and everyone in the room looks at me wearing the same heart-eyes expression on their faces. "It's an adult version of spin the bottle and musical chairs."

I open one of the kitchen drawers in search of a dish towel to tie around my head while everyone listens to the instructions.

"Obviously, since you're all partnered up, I'll be the only one playing this game tonight. But you can all pitch in to help."

I hand the white towel to Lucy and she accepts it with narrowed eyes. "Once the party is in full swing, you cover up my eyes with the towel so I'm blinded and then guide me around the room. When you find someone, I have to kiss the guy of your choosing."

Killer snickers. "Can it be a girl too? That would be hot."

Grace smacks him on the arm. He rears back, rubbing his arm as if injured. "Hey? We're inclusive in this house."

I clear my throat. "Sure, girl or guy, I don't care. But here's how the game continues. Once I've kissed them, I take off the blindfold and get to choose whether I want to keep kissing them the rest of the night or I get to play again."

EJ scratches a hand over his beard. "What if the guy doesn't want to kiss you? Doesn't consent go two ways?"

I snort in laughter, gesturing with my hands out to my side. "Um...hello? Who wouldn't want to kiss me?"

Famous last words.

Chapter Two

Hayes

I slowly walk the two blocks from my new off-campus house to the address I was given.

Joel Henderson, my new quarterback at CFU, invited me to a party at his house, which is apparently called the football house because several of the team members live there. I haven't spent much time with my teammates yet since I literally just pulled into town two days ago. But they seem nice enough and interested in including me in their pre-semester party. It'll be a good way to help me get to know them. I hate being the *new guy*.

Especially since I'm the team's newest kicker and I'm transferring mid-year, post-season. The timing isn't great, but it's the deal I worked out with the coach.

As we're in the off-season, the team meetings are brief and it's all weight room and cardio training and a few scrimmages later this spring.

As a kicker, all of that looks different for me. I don't need to plow guys over on the field; I just need to kick a football with incredible accuracy, to ensure I hit the mark inside the goal post during the most intense periods of the game.

God, it's hard to believe how much my life has changed in the last year.

Never in a million years would I have thought I'd be on a college football team as their kicker. That's because I've always played soccer. My brother, Holden, was the one into football, while soccer has been my life since I was seven years old and I still love playing it.

Life, however, had other ideas. And it was due to a giant tragic twist of fate that I'm now going to be out on the football field instead of the soccer field this coming season.

Guilt washes over me as I think about all the things that have led me to this very moment, and I swallow back the sadness that threatens to overwhelm me almost every minute of the day. It consumes me at times, but not as much as it does Holden. At least I can make the choice to be here. Holden and Kevin, our best friend, can't.

I push those dark thoughts aside and work to clear my mind of all the mistakes I've made. Being here at CFU is my chance to start over. It's the reason I came to campus early so I can start this new life ASAP and find ways to cover up the pain that continually infiltrates my life. I'm no longer the same person I was before the accident because it made me a different person. It turned me into someone I barely recognize anymore.

Maybe, here at CFU, where no one knows about my past, I can pretend it never happened. It may allow me to finally forget about what happened and move on.

As if...

I groan at my own stupidity. I'll never forget it or everything that has happened since then. As a result of those bad decisions, I know I'm left carting this albatross around my neck for eternity.

With a long sigh, I look down the street as I approach a block of older Craftsman-style homes and hear the makings of a good party. It's not overly loud, but I can still hear the bass of the music thumping from inside and mingled voices that penetrate the otherwise quiet night. I'm surprised their neighbors don't complain. Or maybe that's an upside to living in a college town. People must be used to college students and their loud parties around here.

That's one of the aspects of transferring to CFU I'm excited about. The school is just big enough for me to blend into the crowd. No one will talk about me. No one will whisper things as I walk by. They won't say, *"Hey, isn't that the guy whose twin brother was injured and can't play ball anymore? Poor kid."*

I'm a newbie, a nobody here, and I like that. The thought has my spine growing straighter as I turn onto the path up to the three-story house with its sharp roof lines and giant single window on what I assume is an attic room. The lights are all on inside and I can make out the outlines of people dancing and talking on the first floor.

This is good. I can be normal for a few minutes and forget about everything I regret. I need this. I smile to myself for the first time in a long while.

I walk up the slick cement steps, holding the handrail as I do to keep from slipping. Being from Colorado, I'm used to the cold winters and snow, but this wind is another story. I cinch up my hoodie drawstring to keep the cold at bay as I notice three guys sitting in chairs at the far end of the covered porch talking in low voices. I can make out red Solo cups in their hands. One guy has a woman sitting on his lap, his arm protectively around her. For a split second, I feel that immense grief build again, drowning my mind like a tsunami.

I give my head a little shake and look again at the door that's partially ajar, light from inside drifting out in a stream over the porch entry.

Hendy had told me to just come on inside when I got here, and from the sound of it, no one would hear me knocking anyway, even if I did. Taking a deep inhale, I slowly push the door open and expel the air as I step inside.

Before I can even get a good look around and take in my surroundings, I hear the nickname I've been dubbed being shouted out across the room. It's an abbreviated twist on my last name of McIntyre.

"Mac's here!"

"Hey, Mackey! Come on in and join us."

I recognize a few of the new teammates I've already met sprawled out on a sofa and oversized chair in the living room and I smile. The furnishings, while they look comfortable, still appear to have seen better days. Pretty standard for your typical college dwelling. No one wants nice things because they'll just end up getting trashed at parties like this.

A quick scan as I move farther into the room provides me a glimpse at more well-used furniture, a large-screen television currently being used for video gaming, red Solo cups and beer cans everywhere, and a dining area now converted into a semi-dance floor. There's a kitchen to my right with a bunch of people at a long counter mixing drinks with enough alcoholic beverages to qualify as a full-on bar. The lights are all dimmed and somewhere inside there must be a disco ball hanging from the ceiling because sparkly lights reflect on the wall behind the sofa.

There are enough boxes of pizza piled up on a kitchen

table to feed an army and my stomach growls at the smell of food, reminding me I didn't eat lunch today. I got too busy unpacking my suitcases to do anything more than drink a can of Coke. I reach into a bag of chips left open on the coffee table and pop some in my mouth, glancing around to see if I can recognize more of my teammates.

"Hey, Hendy," I say with a small nod of my chin when I see my new QB's head pop up from the sofa, a game controller in his hand. I smile and continue to nervously chew the salty chips before swallowing them down, wishing I had a drink. The whole school and team transfer post-season have me incredibly anxious on how quickly I'll fit in with the team and I wonder how they perceive me. I don't have the long-standing friendships the guys have developed or the close bond teammates have when they've played together for years.

And I'm sure the minute they hear I've never played football on a college team, they are going to think twice about me. Yet something tells me they'll be cool because they seem like they're a good crew of guys who are excited for my arrival.

"Glad you're here, Mac. You play?" Hendy asks as he holds up a black controller in his hands, waving it around for me to see. "We have this new game we just got today. Just be on the lookout for Gracie...she looks all sweet and innocent, but that girl will fucking kick your ass in this game."

Hendy turns back toward the TV with a laugh and I chuckle, having no idea what game he's talking about or who Gracie is. Maybe it's his girlfriend? My gaze follows in the direction of the screen. "Oh, sweet. I didn't even know this came out today. I thought it was scheduled for next weekend."

Hendy snorts. "Me too. Had I known, I wouldn't have invited everyone over to party tonight."

Not having much else to add, I glance behind me and find a spot on one of the wooden chairs set up by the sofa. I take a seat and mindlessly watch the game sequence until a very loud squeal to my right draws my attention. I stand in an attempt to figure out what's happening and whip my head in the direction of the sound.

A blonde-haired girl wearing a white kitchen towel over her eyes is shoved in front of me by another shorter dark-haired chick who exclaims, "This one!"

Before I have a chance to react or move out of the way, the blonde-haired girl blindly lifts her arms and extends them toward my face. She feels around, her hands warm as she places them on my cheeks. In my confusion, I remain motionless, my head trapped between her hands and then the girl leans down to kiss me. Smack on the lips.

What the hell kind of party is this where a woman just blindly kisses a stranger?

That was my first thought. The second one, however, becomes scattered and blown to smithereens when the kiss quickly turns bold. I'm no longer caught off-guard, and I'm enveloped in a vaguely familiar scent that reminds me of Paris in summer.

Lavender and honey.

Her taste, her scent, and the incredible warmth from her is surreal. I drop back into my chair, bringing her with me. The kiss has me in somewhat of a dreamlike state. She swings both arms around my neck and seals her lips over mine almost possessively. Like she's a woman on a mission determined to succeed with her plans. My mouth opens to offer more and a moan slips free from her throat.

And that's when I know.

Holy shit.

This must be a hallucination.

The scent. The sound. The way her lips coast over mine like she can't get enough.

My body instinctively reacts on its own accord before my brain completely catches up with what's going on. If this is a dream, I don't want it to end. I wrap my arms around her waist and tug her into me, her breasts mashing into my chest as my lips lay claim once again to hers.

When my tongue sweeps inside her mouth and I flick the tip over her silver tongue-piercing, she suddenly goes still.

She drops her arms and scrambles off my lap to her feet and takes a step back. Her hands fumble with the kitchen towel, whipping it off her face, staring at me with wide eyes. She blinks. I blink.

Once.

Twice.

She cocks her head to the side and looks around as if confused about where she is. Her gaze returns to me and she stares at me like she's seeing a ghost.

And I return the disbelieving look.

Holy fucking shit. It *is* her.

It's Kelsie Dannon.

I'm not just imagining it and this is not some dream.

Kelsie Dannon is right in front of me.

The same girl I left waiting for me in Paris on Christmas Eve and have regretted doing it ever since.

I never expected to see her again. How could we? We only used our prepaid French numbers while there and never exchanged our U.S. phone numbers or talked about where we went to school.

We left everything open and casual, just like she wanted it to be.

Yet here she is and it's not even my subconscious wishing we were together in the same place again, wrapped up in each other's kisses.

This is fucking real. But... oh, shit...fuck my life. I watch her expression morph from dazed and confused with the initial shock of seeing me to livid, her eyes shooting daggers.

Panic rises in my throat and I swallow it down, having the presence of mind to look contrite. I watch as anger flushes over her face, a deepening red tinting her cheekbones, and I know she's pissed as hell at me right now for what I did to her in Paris.

She has every right to never want to speak to me again.

Or read me the fucking riot act.

And if I know Kelsie, she's about to do just that.

That guilt I carried with me when I walked in the door tonight washes over me with a vengeance, coating every molecule of my body. This is bad. So very, *very* bad.

Denim blue eyes narrow on me, turning a deep sea blue and I extend my hand to her, whether it's for protection or to reach out in case she tries to bolt. But she doesn't. Instead, in a cold, dismissive voice she says, "You *fucking* bastard."

And then before I can duck or dodge, her hand whips out and slaps me hard across my cheek, leaving a hot sting in its wake. My head snaps back instinctively, but I don't get up. I rub a palm over the skin that's burning with a dull pain.

But I know it's nothing compared to the pain I caused her. I stand as I attempt to formulate a response, but my mind draws a blank.

Some dude behind her says, "Whoa, Kels! What's the deal? Did this guy try something on you?"

She ignores the comment of concern with a scoff and all the gawkers in the room have stopped talking and turned their attention to this highly-unusual confrontation.

"I don't know what the fuck you're doing here, but you can get the fuck out right now!" she seethes, trying to side-step past me, throwing the bandana on the floor like it's just done something to offend her. My gaze tracks her as she spins on her heel, ready to make a break for it, but my hand snaps out to snag her wrist. My mind swirls as I uncon-sciously rub the spot on my cheek, holding her in place so I can talk to her.

The big guy who steps in, Killer, offers a protective gesture when he puts a hand up to my chest, his gaze darting between me and Kelsie, who wiggles free from my grasp. "Do you two know each other or something?"

Hendy drops his controller on the couch and stands up. Both guys are obviously ready to intervene on behalf of their friend, if necessary. And regardless of whether I'm their new teammate or not, it's very clear whose side they'd be on if it turns out I'm the villain in this situation.

Let's face it, I kind of am.

"Uh, dude, it's pretty fucking clear they know each other," Hendy adds with a snort as Kelsie gives me a death glare that could kill a lesser man if that man wasn't already fueled by pain and regret.

I reach out for her again to prevent her from leaving, but Hendy steps between us.

"Let her go, bro."

She snarls at me, "You don't ever fucking touch me again..."

She doesn't finish her thought because one of her

friends pulls her toward the kitchen and out of my reach, but not out of earshot. Hendy is still in my way, arms crossed over his chest, offering his protective support of Kelsie.

Fuck. This was not the way I saw this party going tonight. I was here to make friends and now all I've done is create a scene.

"Grace, let me go. If he stays, I'm leaving." She practically spits out her words, angrily pointing her finger back at me.

"What is going on right now? Who is this guy?" another girl asks, her gaze ping-ponging between Kelsie and me, concern stitched in her furrowed brows.

Hendy, now more than a little concerned over what's happening, stares at me judgingly. "Mac, what did you do to her to make her so mad, bro?"

I suck in a breath. That's a loaded question that I'm not sure can be answered succinctly. The answer has a level of complexity I can't even begin to explain.

All I know is that I've come face to face again with the woman I fell in love with just weeks ago. A woman I was sure I'd never run into again...because I'm an idiot.

Kelsie jerks her arm free from her friend and runs toward the front door before anyone can stop her, slamming it behind her.

Shit! I take off in the same direction, pushing past Hendy and the small crowd of onlookers as I open the front door and run outside.

Hendy and Killer join me.

"You all right, Kels?" Hendy yells.

"Your coat!" Killer adds, tossing a purple coat in her direction.

"I'm fine. Just go," Kelsie replies as she catches the coat and takes off across their front yard.

"Kelsie! Please, wait!" I call out after her as I sprint to catch up.

She stops abruptly at the corner of the street and whips around, pointing an accusatory finger at me. I stop short, leaving space between us in case she tries to slap me again. I'm breathing hard, both from the run and my anxious thoughts.

"No, I don't think so," she says firmly, her voice rising with every word. "You don't get to explain, Hayes. I don't want to hear anything from those lying, betraying lips of yours. You had your chance and you blew it. So stay the fuck away from me. I don't know why you're here or how you found me, but I never want to see you again."

I open my mouth, but she takes off running again into the night. I lose sight of her as she cuts through a yard, snow flying around her. Damn, she is one fast runner. Maybe she's on the track team?

I wouldn't know because I have no insight into who Kelsie is outside of the girl I fell for in Paris.

We chose not to share anything about each other's lives and now I regret all of that.

I regret everything except for meeting her.

As I stare down the street after her, I shake my head over the night's events.

So much for new starts and forgetting my past mistakes.

Because the second worst mistake I ever made was leaving the woman I loved with just a text of goodbye.

The irony is that while the universe has offered me an open door for a possible reconciliation.

Kelsie just slammed it right in my face.

Chapter Three

K elsie

I run as far and as fast as I can, not caring about the snow or the cold, or the fact that instead of wearing my brand new coat, I'm clutching it in my arms like a damn fool.

Nothing else matters right now except getting as far away from Hayes McIntyre as humanly possible.

The vibration in my pocket alerts me to the dozens of messages currently blowing up my phone. I'd bet a million dollars they are all from Lucy and Grace wondering what the fuck is going on right now.

I'd pay to know that too.

Why the hell was Hayes at our house party tonight?

Why isn't he back in Colorado where he told me he lived?

God, I'm such a fool. It's my fault I was so easily blinded by this guy. It was my idea not to share anything except the bare essentials with each other while we were together. I thought that would make it easier when we left Paris.

I assumed if I didn't know much about him, I couldn't get attached and then miss him when he left.

Stupid fucking idea.

My damn heart didn't care whether I knew many personal details about Hayes. It fell anyway.

My mind retreats back to all the time we spent together during our semester abroad. We lived in the moment. Enjoyed each other's company in the here and now, not allowing our lives back home to interfere with what we had going on together in Paris.

It was just supposed to be a fling that would fizzle out.

Only it didn't.

Fuck, how did I fall so hopelessly in love with a guy I trusted so blindly and now I'm paying the price?

Stupid. Stupid. Stupid.

I kick off the snow from my boots against the steps of the house, shivering from the cold wind as I enter in my key code on the door pad.

Due to the fact that I lived abroad last semester, I didn't have a place to come back to on campus since both my best friends are now shacking up with their SOs in the football house. So I was forced to find other accommodations with a short-term lease this semester. Luckily, I'd stayed in touch with my friend Parker Lange, one of my student partners from my entrepreneurship class last year, while I was in France. She'd told me that two rooms were available in the home her father owns and rents out and that I could sublease one.

I chose the only bedroom on the main floor in the back of the house that has its own bathroom. It's perfect. I moved in and love the view from the small but cozy room that looks out over a nature preserve and the mountains to the west.

It's not the luxurious flat I lived in that looked out over Montmartre in Paris, but I'll manage and it will offer me the space I need to study.

Entering the second door into the house and then the front hallway, I toe off my wet boots to leave them by the door, where I see a few other pairs of shoes all lined up against the wall. Parker said there are five housemates, including herself, and I've only met one of them so far. Her name is Eleanor and she's a graduate student.

I walk down the long hallway, past the stairs that lead up to the second and third floors, and unlock my bedroom door, swinging it open to find boxes still left to unpack.

At least my bed is made. Throwing myself across the comforter, I pluck out my phone, reading through the urgent texts that have come through since I raced out of the house.

> Grace: KELSIE! Come back. Tell us what happened.

> Lucy: What the heck just happened? Where are you? How do you know Mac?

> Grace: Tell us where you are so we can talk.

> Grace: SUGAR SMACKS…we are going to hunt you down if you don't call us ASAP!!!

> Lucy: Holy shit…I just heard Mac tell Hendy he's the same Hayes you met in Paris.

Lucy: OMG Kelsie...I can't even! I don't care that he's the new kicker for the team, that guy is never ever being invited to our house EVER again.

Grace: Plz just tell us you're okay. We're coming over now.

I groan and set my phone on the bed before squishing my face into my pillow and punching the mattress a few times with my fist in pent-up frustration.

That's not all I want to punch right now.

I wish I would've slapped Hayes harder in the face. Or, better yet, kicked him in the balls.

I'm not normally prone to violent outbursts. Although I am known for my fiery personality and quick-fuse temper, which I often turn into dramatic passive-aggressive storming off behavior. Yeah, I'm not proud of those traits, but that's who I am. So coming face to face with the guy that ripped my heart to shreds and ghosted me certainly brought out the worst in me tonight.

I roll over to my side when I hear the buzzer on the front door. Almost simultaneously my phone lights up with a call.

I swipe to answer, seeing Grace's face on the lock screen. "I'm coming. Hold on."

Trudging down the hallway, I unlock the old Victorian style, floor-to-ceiling door and step out into the vestibule to open the second door.

The girls come rushing in, ready to be my support as they both wrap their arms around me in a tackle hug, talking a mile a minute.

"We're here for you, babes," Lucy says in a sweet whisper-soft murmur. "And we will rip his ball hairs off one by one if he tries to weasel his way back into your life."

I snort-laugh at Lucy's sweet-as-honey voice using such menacing words.

"Yeah," Grace interjects. "And we can break his legs too. He can't play ball here without them, right?"

"For fuck's sake, who knew you two were such ball crushers? Jesus, remind me never to get on either one of your bad sides. You are pure evil hidden under angelic looks."

They both laugh and then give each other concerned looks before taking off their coats and boots, hanging their outerwear on the hook rack in the vestibule. Once down to their stocking feet, they follow me into the main sitting room and common area where, thankfully, it's completely quiet.

Because the semester doesn't begin until January 15th, the house is fairly empty. Of the five bedrooms, Eleanor and I are the only ones here this week. Although, I think I heard someone moving in and then coming and going the last two days. I haven't met them yet because I was busy in my room, but I'm sure we'll run into each other soon.

I flop down on the worn-out brown leather couch and the girls flank me on either side, each grabbing onto my hands and wiggling their fingers through mine. I consider where to start.

"We might need booze for this," I joke and clutch Lucy's hand when she starts to get up to head to the kitchen. I pull her back down and she sits with a plop. "I'm kidding. I mean, we can drink afterwards, but I'm so upset right now I think if I got drunk, I'd do something stupid."

Grace's eyes light up deviously. "Like what? Put something on socials about his tiny dick?"

I sputter out a laugh and shake my head. "Sadly, that would be a complete lie. It's true what they say about shoe size."

Lucy's mouth drops open and she coughs into her hand. "Hmm...same thing about their hands. Emmett has *really* big hands and long fingers."

She sighs and we all collapse into each other in a fit of laughter as Grace joins in on our ridiculous interpretation of the old wives' tales about penis size.

"If that's the case, Killer is one big *boned* man!"

"He has a killer boner!"

We continue giggling and my initial anger and shock begins to dissipate now that my friends have shown up to remind me that I'm loved.

When we finally get all the jokes out of our systems, the tone returns to a more serious nature when I open up about my feelings toward Hayes.

"I've never felt so hurt and heartbroken over a guy before," I say, my chin quivering as I try to keep back the sobs. "I'm sorry for not confiding in you about all of this before, but I wanted to forget about it because it hurt so much. When he left me in Paris, I felt so unwanted and alone. I was so embarrassed because he dumped me."

Lucy wraps an arm around me and Grace squeezes my hand in hers. My friends surround me with their love and support, grounding me in a way nobody ever has since my brother and my aunt.

"Kelsie, you are never alone. We've got you, girl," Lucy says, snuggling her face against my arm. "And everyone loves you because you're our Kelsie."

While I'd love to believe that's true, I know it's a lie. If it were true, then why did Hayes leave me like I meant nothing to him?

Grace adds in her two cents. "Listen, Kels, we've all been through it. God, it hurts so much. It's why they call it heartbreak."

I give a sad smile at Grace. She knows more than anyone how it feels to lose someone close. She's gone through a lot with her own mother, just as I have with my brother and parents.

I straighten my shoulders and stand up, brushing off the sadness as I head into the kitchen to dig out the bottles I'd stashed when I moved in.

"Okay, it's time to get drunk."

I give both girls a look over my shoulder and make them a promise. "But this time, there will be no kissing games."

And I silently vow to myself never to kiss Hayes McIntyre ever again.

Chapter Four

Hayes

I check my phone for the third time today. I've been up since five this morning. It's another winter training day for the football team to keep in shape for our spring games that start in only a few more weeks.

We might only have a handful of scrimmages starting in March, but if I'm going to make this work, I need to be ready. I've never had this kind of pressure on me when I was out on the soccer field because I was a midfielder. I had the team around me and we jointly had responsibility for the ball.

Now, as a kicker, all eyes are on me when the time comes. It's my sole responsibility to ensure my kicks are accurate.

I press my feet against the platform on the machine and grunt as I lift several hundred pounds with my legs. Returning the weight to the ready position, I relax as I hear the clang of the weights dropping at the machine next to me.

"Shit, bro. That's a lot of weight," Hendy says with a whistle.

I pat my quads and laugh. "Well, I didn't get these from just jumping rope, I can tell you that."

Since I no longer have to be counted on to run, I've felt the need to bulk up even more now that I'm playing football. With soccer, I wanted lean muscles and stamina in order to sustain myself on a field for the duration of the game, but not with football. Here, I need to have muscle and reliability. God, I hope I can pull this off.

This was never my dream, but apparently the universe decided to dictate the trajectory of my life.

And who the hell knew that by doing so I'd have met Kelsie and then found her again at this college. Fucking universe has a maniacal sense of humor.

"I can't wait to see you out on the field when we start regular spring practices after the break," Hendy says with a grin as he slings a towel over his shoulder. "We'll see if those calves and quads of yours live up to the hype."

He snaps me with the towel across my thigh with a chuckle and then strides off to the PT room. It's a bummer I won't be playing officially with these guys next fall because most of them will be graduating in the spring.

This coming fall will be my first season as a kicker. It gives me anxiety that none of my teammates know I've never played on a football team before. Only Coach knows of my lack of experience because he's the one who recruited me through a series of discussions with my former soccer coach. He brought me in during this semester to begin training with the team during our spring sessions and also has most of the graduating players staying on through the end of the semester.

Coach had seen me play soccer by happenstance when

he came to Colorado to watch his nephew play on an opposing team. He came up to me afterward and inquired about my interest in playing football. I thought he was nuts, but after further discussion and after determining whether or not I was even eligible, Coach offered me a kicker position to start this year.

It was Holden who encouraged me to take him up on the recruitment offer. And out of a sense of obligation to my brother, who could never play again and said he'd never pass up an opportunity like this, I accepted.

And here I am.

My phone pings and I look down.

> Holden: I'm fine. Stop mothering me. No, actually, you're way worse than Mom.

I smile sadly. Although it seems like he's having a good day today with his banter and humorous response, that can change from minute to minute. His mood swings are difficult to anticipate and have put a strange division in our relationship.

> Me: Dude, there is no way I'm worse than Mom. Remember that time she wanted to tape the thermometer to your forehead after surgery?

I see the three little dots and I wait.

> Holden: True. Okay, I concede. Stop Dadding me.

I chuckle loudly and draw the attention of another guy across the room. Reading his funny reply lifts my own mood.

It's as though I'm talking to the former version of my

brother, my twin who was once fun and carefree. The guy who wouldn't take shit from anyone and always made me laugh.

God, I miss that person.

> Me: Fair enough. You win.

> Holden: No shit I win. Your attempt to win was pathetic. What the hell are you even learning at CFU?

> Me: Oh, wait… I'm supposed to learn something here?

> Holden: Yeah, something like that.

> Me: Noted.

I slip my phone in my gym shorts pocket and walk over to the only open treadmill along the wall of the fitness room. Time to cool down.

Next to me on my right is Killian, the big dude everyone calls Killer. I can see why that name is fitting. I bet he kills it out on the field as the tight end. He has earbuds in his ears, but when I step onto the machine, I give him a nod of hello and start a light jog, increasing my pace to keep up with him. Once I'm there, he pulls a bud out of his ear and greets me with an easy smile. For such a massive brute of a guy, he's pretty laidback and nice. And he didn't punch me the other night for what happened between Kelsie and me. That's saying something.

"Hey bro," he says, slowing down his pace a little. "You ready for classes this week, FNG?"

"FNG?"

He claps me on the back with a laugh. "Yeah, you know. Fucking new guy."

I chuckle because I've never heard anyone say that to me before. Maybe because I've never been the fucking new guy.

"I guess so. At least I was able to get in most of the classes I wanted to take. I was a little worried because a few of my credits didn't transfer from my previous school, which means next year I'll have to take more. That'll suck, since I'll have senioritis," I answer, slowing the machine down to a slower jog.

"Yeah. I feel ya there. We're all seniors this year and I'm fucking lucky with the independent study classes I have. I can coast into graduation," Killer says with a broad grin, gesturing with the swoop of his arm. He glances over at me. "So, where'd you play ball before this?"

I falter a little with my steps and wipe my brow. I decide to keep it low-key and generic to avoid the topic of my soccer playing versus football. "Colorado."

"Cool. I'm from Iowa. Got any siblings?" he asks, as if we're just shooting the shit and not getting through a workout. What the hell type of twenty questions is this?

"A brother," I answer a little hesitantly, wishing my time was counting down faster.

"Younger or older?"

Shit. I always hate answering this one. Now that everything's happened between me and Holden, it's even more complex. It just adds more questions that I don't want to answer.

"We're twins, actually," I say a little reluctantly, glancing at the dashboard timer on my treadmill. Two more minutes to go.

"No way! That's so cool, man. What's that like? Are you identical? Do you have that twin-to-twin telepathy shit or something?"

Killer suddenly stops walking, taking the other bud out of his ear and turning his full attention on me as if I'm some kind of circus animal. It's always like this. I could probably guess his next five questions.

One will definitely be if we have our own language and because he's a college dude, he'll ask if we've ever shared a girl.

He leans in and whispers conspiratorially, "Ever shared a girl?"

Nailed it. If only I had a dollar for every time I get these questions, I'd be a freaking millionaire.

"No. We don't really have the same type."

"Oh, bummer. How about a secret language?" he prods.

And there it is.

"Nah. Not that either." If we did, maybe I could help my brother out of his darkness. Instead, I have to just sit back and watch as he continues to spiral.

My timer beeps on the machine and I thank the time gods for the interruption so I can leave this awkward conversation behind. "Well, off to shower. I'll talk to you later."

"Sure. See you later, Mac," Killer says with a wave, but then hesitates before latching onto my arm to stop me. I glance over my shoulder at him.

"Yeah?"

He clears his throat. "Hey, I don't know what the deal is with you and Kelsie Dannon, but be careful there. She's one of us, ya know?"

The warning is clear—don't fuck with her or I'll be sorry.

I nod my head. "Got it. Thanks."

I hurry into the locker room to shower and dress so I can get back to my place to finish putting together the bookshelf I bought.

Although I was told the room was furnished when I rented it online, I found it was a little lacking for what I needed. Overall, though, the house is quiet, close to campus, and although I have to share a bathroom with someone, it's right next door to my bedroom, so there's at least that.

I've never had to share anything with anyone else besides Holden. This will be a unique experience. I was told I get one shelf in the fridge and one cabinet in the kitchen, but I'm free to use the kitchen anytime I like. There's also a decent size television and sofa in the family room and the back yard is actually pretty nice. There's a big deck, a hot tub, and even a fire pit that all looks out over the mountains and nature preserve.

It reminds me a lot of home. Whether that's a good thing or not is yet to be determined.

I've finished getting ready and I'm just about to leave when Hendy notices me and waves me over. He's pulling a sweatshirt over his head that reads CFU Football.

"Hey, Mac, a few of us are grabbing breakfast at the diner on Main Street after this if you want to come along," he offers.

Shit, I do and I don't. I appreciate that our team captain is making an effort to include me on things off the field, given what went down the other night with one of his friends. But he seems to have moved on from that and accepted me into the fold.

Or it could be one of those situations of keeping your friends close and your enemies closer.

I consider his offer and sling my bag over my shoulder.

"Yeah, that'd be cool. I can stop by for a few minutes. Then I gotta get my place sorted out. It's a mess."

Hendy laughs like what I said is funny. "Dude, you're in college. It's supposed to be a mess!"

I open the locker room door and he follows me out. Once in the hallway, he throws an arm around my shoulder and I instinctively know what's coming next.

The talk.

"So, what's up with you and Kelsie?" he asks, not in the same serious tone Killer used, but the implication is still there. I get it. They're protective over their girl and I think that's cool. She has good friends in them.

Although I don't really want to talk about things until I clear the air with Kelsie, I also can't shut him down either. That'd be rude when I'm the new guy and trying to make friends with him and my teammates.

"Yeah. Kelsie and I happened to be in Paris in the same program last semester," I answer, trying to keep my explanation as short as possible and leave it fairly open-ended. He's a smart guy. I'm sure he can connect the dots and figure out Kelsie and I hooked up.

He whistles again, raising an eyebrow. "Kelsie's a tough one, dude. She's hot as fuck, but does her own thing. No one around campus—not even me—has been able to tame that one. She's like those wild horses you hear about. She doesn't let many get close to her. If she likes you, she *really* likes you. If not, she'll fucking let you know it."

I'm not sure if he's trying to make me feel better or not. What does come as a relief is that it sounds like Hendy never slept with Kelsie.

I feel my jaw unclench and my hands relax. Or did he hook up with her? If so, I want to flatten him to the ground.

"Um, did you guys hook up or something?"

Hendy stops and turns to me, looking me over as if deciding whether to trust me or not. His lips finally curve up at the corners. "Nah, not that way. We're just good friends. But don't tell anyone that because I have a reputation to keep," he says with a laugh as we turn a corner and walk up the steps to the diner. "But God help the guy who finally captures that girl. She will take him for the ride of his life and probably buck him off before she finally gives in all the way."

I grab the handle and open the door to the diner, allowing Hendy to walk in before me as I follow behind, considering what he said. Am I the first guy she's had a relationship with? Am I the guy who captured her heart?

If so, the thought has me both brimming with confidence and feeling the massive remorse of hurting her.

"Hey, Sherrie!" Hendy calls out to a woman behind the counter as we enter the restaurant. "A full breakfast for me and my friend here will have..."

"Oh, uh, can I get a bagel with eggs, bacon, and cheddar to go, please?" I ask.

"Sure thing, sugar," Sherrie says. "Coming right up."

Hendy takes a spot in a booth and I slide in on the other side to wait for my to-go order. Sherrie stops over with a pot of coffee, filling up the empty cup in front of Hendy and looking to me for confirmation. I shake my head.

As she walks away, Hendy takes a sip and then lifts his brows at me.

"Just so you know, it sounds like Kelsie is pretty pissed at you and things could get a little complicated because both Killer and EJ date her best friends."

Nodding slowly, I try to figure out where he's going

with this. I toy with the napkin sitting on the table as he continues.

"I'd hate to have to ban you from the football house, but the girls are threatening us to do it."

He shakes his head and then gives a wave to a few other players who walk into the diner and then get seated a few tables away.

"Were you and Kelsie *together* together in Paris?" he asks, as something flashes in his eyes. Is it jealousy? Or just concern?

Before I can respond, Sherrie returns to our table with a small paper bag in hand. "Your sandwich."

I toss down a ten. "Thanks, Sherrie. I'll probably be here for dinner again too."

"Anytime, son."

I scoot out of the seat to exit the booth, thankful that the food was ready so quickly and we don't have to continue this conversation.

"So...is she yours?" Hendy asks, grabbing my arm before I leave.

I want to laugh at the complexity of that question. I want to scream, *"Yes, she's mine and I want her back!'"*

But, instead, I simply shake my head and say, "No."

Because she's not mine anymore and probably never will be again.

"Good to know. Take it easy, bro."

I nod and walk out with my breakfast in hand even though I don't feel the least bit hungry. Suddenly, I'm left wondering how many guys Kelsie has been with. I know it shouldn't matter because we're not together, but it still stabs at my gut. I need to get back to my place so I can decompress and turn off my thoughts for a few minutes.

Hell, I don't want to think about anything, especially

who she may or may not have hooked up with besides me. I just want to do a mindless activity for a few minutes and avoid having thoughts of Kelsie roaming free in my head.

Buttoning up my coat and throwing my hoodie over my head, I walk down the tree-lined street the three blocks from the diner and end up at the big, old house I'm calling home this semester.

As I attempt to enter the four-digit code into the keypad while juggling my breakfast in my other hand, I let out a sigh of relief when out of the corner of my eye I see someone opening up the interior vestibule door and then the exterior. I lift my eyes, ready to introduce myself to one of my housemates and say thanks, when my gaze lands on the last person I expect to see.

The next ten seconds happen as if in slow motion.

In front of me on the threshold of the doorway, looking hot as fuck, stands Kelsie. She has on a pair of bright pink leggings and a cropped black top with sports bra straps showing from under the neckline. Her hair is piled high on her head in a ponytail and she wears a pair of earpods.

Because her eyes are cast down at her phone as she fiddles with it, she hasn't noticed me standing here yet. But the minute she slips the phone into a pocket in her leggings and raises her head, her eyes meet mine and we both freeze.

We stand three feet apart from one another, but I swear I can hear her heartbeat loud and clear. She's a step above me, putting her nearly at my eye level. I watch those big blue eyes grow wide from shock and a myriad of other emotions.

Until she yanks an earbud from her ear and anger creases her forehead, her mouth slanting in a frown. "What the hell are you doing here, Hayes?"

"Kelsie?" I ask, incredibly confused as to why she's

leaving my house. I point stupidly at the door behind her. "I live here."

She blanches. "Bullshit. No, you don't. I live here," she says, pointing to herself.

Well, shit on a brick.

Things just got a whole lot more awkward.

Chapter Five

K elsie

"You've got to be fucking kidding me," I lament as I stare at Hayes, who has climbed the remaining steps to the front door and is now face to face with me.

I was just leaving for my 10 a.m. yoga session at the student fitness center where I'm meeting Grace and Lucy. Looks like I'm going to need a helluva lot more than some deep breathing and *shavasan* poses to deal with this new revelation.

How is it possible that my ex-lover is now living in the same house as me?

Hayes gives me an apologetic shrug, his eyes cast down to his feet. "This is pretty weird, right?"

"Yeah," I grunt, letting out a haughty huff. "You can say that again. Guess you'll be looking for a new place to live."

I dismiss him with a wave of my hand, brushing past

him down to the top step, securing my yoga mat strap over my shoulder. I'm stopped when he tugs me back, halting my quick escape with a firm hand on my arm.

"Uh, I'm not moving. I just moved in."

Snapping my head around, I stare at him in defiance, yanking my arm free from his grasp. "Uh...not my problem. I was here first so you need to leave."

To my surprise, Hayes doubles over in a fit of laughter. He laughs so hard he has to place the bag he was carrying on the ground and holds himself up with one palm on his thigh and the other wrapped around his stomach.

I stare at him in indignation. "What the fuck is so funny right now?"

When his laughter dies down, he lifts his torso and shakes his head. "You don't find this whole situation funny, Kels? I mean, what are the chances that we'd not only end up at the same school but also in the same house?" He sputters through a chuckle. "And you can probably bet dollars to donuts we'll be in some of the same classes too."

I pin him with a murderous glare and straighten my back. "If so, I guess you'll not only be moving out but also switching programs."

He hoots out again and crosses his arms over his chest. "Not happening. I'm here for the semester and committed to the football team. You'll just have to put on your big girl panties and deal with my presence like a grownup."

I'm seething inside now. How dare he suggest I'm anything but mature?

"Ha! That's rich coming from the immature asshole who left me without a word on Christmas Eve. Yeah, that was so grown up of you, Hayes."

Something shifts in his expression and his eyes turn soft. God, those eyes of his could melt me into a puddle. Warm brown honey and amber. Add that to his beautiful smile and the thick dark hair that's always a bit shaggy, it all reminds me why I fell so hard for him in Paris.

But that was then and this is now and I will not be fooled again.

"Kelsie, I know I owe you an explanation. I didn't mean to hurt you like that when I left Paris." He tries to reach out and touch my arm again, but I flinch away. "I had my reasons and none of them had to do with you. I swear."

I glance away, fighting off the tears wanting to spill out as I stare down the front path that's now covered by a light dusting of snow. As if my body just realized how cold it is in only my yoga gear, I shiver and wrap my arms around my middle.

"I don't care about your reasons, Hayes. You did what you did and I'm not going to forgive and forget. The best you're going to get from me is my middle finger and my ass as I walk away."

I swing around and march down the steps. I throw my hand in the air and give him my middle finger while smacking my butt cheek, which I know for certain looks amazing in these leggings. "Bite me, asshole."

He mutters something that I can't hear because I'm already shoving my earbuds back in my ears and jogging down the street.

If anyone is in need of a stress-relieving yoga session today, it's me.

By the time I make it to the studio, I'm already five minutes later than I'd planned because I had to stop and catch my breath before entering the building. My body is hyped up on the adrenaline that kicked in when I learned that one of my new housemates is my former fling.

I inhale deeply and open the door to the studio, toeing

off my shoes and leaving them in the cubby at the front before entering the fairly crowded room. I'm immediately greeted by Grace flapping her arm in the air to wave me over.

"We saved a spot for you," she says with a proud smile.

"Thanks." I unroll my mat and place my water bottle on the floor next to it, avoiding Grace and Lucy's gazes. I'm afraid if I look at them, they'll see everything that's swirling around in my head.

I just need to get through this class and let out all this pent-up irritation from the last few days.

The problem is I'm not very good at letting shit go. I tend to hold on to emotional baggage and pack it in tight, letting that grudge fester like an abscessed tooth. Once someone burns me, my trust in them is gone once and for all.

"Is everything okay, Kels?" Lucy whispers, leaning over to talk just as the instructor welcomes the class.

I wave her off and give her a tight smile. "I'm fine. S'all good."

The class begins with *tadasana* and then lengthening our bodies to the sky. The stretch that normally feels so good has me feeling stuck instead of elongated. I have so many questions whirling around my head about Hayes.

Why is he here at CFU?

How did I not know he was a football player? I thought he told me he played soccer?

And how is it possible we're living under the same roof?

All these unanswered questions have my muscles tightening in frustration instead of relaxing.

His reappearance also has me rehashing the time we spent together in Paris. At the time, it was just a fling and I didn't want anything too serious. So we made a pact that we'd live in the present and would only tell each other three things about ourselves, leaving everything else off the table. That way, it was all about the here and now and we wouldn't become attached when it came time to leave.

That day, we'd been sitting outside at a sidewalk cafe just a block from the Louvre, sipping on our coffees and eating pastries while enjoying the gorgeous fall afternoon together.

Hayes reaches over to wipe a crumb from the corner of my lip and I teasingly try to bite him, snapping my teeth at this thumb.

"Why you be hatin'?" he jokes, sticking out his tongue before licking the crumb away.

I waggle my eyebrows suggestively. "You didn't seem to mind my teeth last night."

Hayes closes his eyes and smiles dreamily. "No, I did not. God, Kels. You are so dirty. I'm afraid to ask where you learned that little trick."

He opens his eyes again and looks at me with a more serious expression.

"I feel like I don't know a lot about you."

I grin and flick a strand of hair over my shoulder. "What more do you need to know? I'm hot, young, and I'm good with my tongue."

Hayes chuckles and rolls his eyes but leans over the table to kiss me on the cheek "That's an understatement."

The last two weeks since our first hookup has been the best sex I've had in my whole life. Hayes is an incredibly giving lover, so unlike the guys I've hooked up with back at home. He matches my sense of adventure both in bed and out in the real world. He's fun and witty, sweet and thoughtful.

I usually get bored with a guy after one hookup. But with Hayes, I'm insatiable and want him all the time.

It kind of freaks me out how quickly I've grown attached to him. Which is precisely why I don't want it to get serious.

I scoot my chair closer to his and lift my hand to the side of his head, sifting my fingers through the hair above his ear. It's long and shaggy, and it drives me crazy with desire.

"How about this?" I suggest, leaning in to kiss him, flicking the tip of my tongue over the shell of his ear. "Let's each share three things about ourselves. But nothing about our homes, schools, or families. Will that satisfy your curiosity?"

"Okay, that works," he agrees. "What questions should we answer?"

I tap my finger at my chin. "Hmm...let's start with favorite food."

He grins. "Easy. My grandmother's homemade apple pie. And yours?"

"French pastries." I pop the last bite of my croissant into my mouth and moan.

We barely finish asking the next question before we start making out and soon all the questions are forgotten as we rush back to my flat to make each other orgasm.

As we lie in bed, arms wrapped around our naked and sweaty bodies, the light of dusk streaming through my loft window, Hayes returns to our earlier discussion and asks me the final question.

"Where's your favorite place you've ever been?" His finger lightly traces over the curve of my collarbone and I sigh.

"Right here with you."

Chapter Six

Hayes

I'd be lying if I said I didn't want to run into Kelsie this morning. I don't want to corner her or wait outside her door like a lost puppy or anything, but I want to explain what happened. I really do, but it's difficult.

If I tell her everything...she may never look at me the same way again.

But if I don't, I know with certainty that she'll never forgive me. It's this double-edged sword and I feel like I can't win either way.

I still can't believe the weird twist of fate that she not only attends CFU, but also happens to live in the same freaking house as me.

When I left Paris, I thought it'd be a clean break and we'd never see each other again. That was the plan anyway, and we had both agreed there'd be no contact after we parted.

I thought I was saving myself from the possibility of falling in love, but that was a huge miscalculation on my part. I haven't stopped thinking about her for one minute since I left.

Being in the place I was mentally, I thought it would be better if we both moved on with our lives without a backward glance. I knew I couldn't be the man she needed, especially in a long-distance relationship.

Hell, half the time, I don't know if I can be the man *I* need me to be.

With a drawn-out sigh, I sling my backpack over my shoulder and trudge downstairs to the main floor of the house. The kitchen is empty and I don't hear Kelsie in her room. I know now that she's in the bedroom in the rear of the house. With it being so early, she's probably still sleeping. I remember in Paris she loved to stay up late and work on her art and then would oversleep and be late for our morning classes at the university. When I asked her about it, she said she was a night owl and would often stay up until 2 or 3 a.m. to paint.

I wonder if she still paints in her free time. Does she take art classes in school?

I put those unanswered questions aside and head to class, stopping first at the student union cafe for some coffee.

The minute I step into the domed building foyer, the light streaming in from above, I get in line for my latte and hear my nickname being called out from behind me.

"Boys, it's Mac's big first day!" Killer shouts boisterously as he walks toward me. He throws an arm over my shoulder and smiles broadly. "Dude, are you ready for classes?"

I shrug. "Is anyone ever really ready for class?"

He laughs. "Good point!"

Then he turns around, dropping his arm from me

before reaching for his girlfriend, Grace, nuzzling into her neck as she giggles.

"Good morning, Grace," I greet, hoping to sound friendly and to avoid the stink eye. I know she's one of Kelsie's friends and is clearly on Team Kelsie.

"Hey," she says like I'm a complete stranger before her gaze moves back to her giant boyfriend.

Oh, great. That's not a good start.

I assume that after our interaction at the party the other night, Kelsie gave her friends the download on what happened, in the event they didn't already know.

I'm sure I wear devil horns in their eyes and am a guy not to be bothered with. At least my teammates don't seem to have the same level of animosity toward me.

"Well, we're off." Killer slaps me on the back and the force behind it has me bumping into the girl in line in front of me. She swivels around and gives me a '*WTF*' look. I make my quick apology.

"Sorry."

"Okay, man. Have a good day at school, Mac. Make sure to bring the professor an apple," he teases jovially. "We'll see you later at practice."

I flick him off and he just laughs, the sound carrying throughout the high-domed center room. Then he turns toward Grace, slipping his hand in hers and they head out to talk with some of our other teammates.

If it weren't for my strange encounter with Kelsie and the tension with her friends, I'd feel like I could really belong at CFU. Killer, EJ, and Hendy have all been very welcoming to me, as have the other players. I just hope the same holds true as I begin to meet other students in my classes.

By the time I wait for my drink order, everyone else has

cleared from the front of the building. Although I scoped everything out the other morning when I took a walk around, I still pull up the campus map on my phone to locate my first class. I'm not used to being on such a large campus. Everything here seems so foreign to me.

That brings up the memory of the day I met Kelsie. I've always struggled with directions and maps, and I was at a café in Paris trying to get my bearings, starting down at a city map, when she came up and introduced herself.

God, that seems like a lifetime ago already. And now here I am.

Should I even be here?

The question echoes in my brain like a foghorn as I race toward the Sheridan Building at the far end of the quad. As I enter the building, I glance down at my phone one more time to confirm the location of my first class—Room 115, first floor, just around the corner from the entrance.

I stride down the hallway and see the door to the lecture hall already open and follow another guy inside. Glancing around, I check out the space. It's not one of those huge halls that holds five hundred students or anything, but maybe close to fifty. I scan around for an open seat, noticing about twenty-some students already seated in various chairs, most of them near the front of the room.

I choose a spot close to the middle and pull out my laptop from my bag. Opening it up, I start a new folder labeled *Managing Family Business in an International Marketplace*. It sounded interesting when I registered and checked off a box on my major course requirements.

I'm not yet sure how I'll use my degree when I graduate. Before the accident, I wanted to start a company with my brother and one of our friends. They liked the idea of something tactile. A local, small town business on Main Street, while I dreamed big. I wanted to have offices in different countries. I wanted to have investors and grow something from the ground up that could become important, meaningful to the world. But I was a kid, and what was meaningful changed weekly. We had brainstormed different ideas, but hadn't settled on one yet, when the accident happened.

A friend had gone to Paris that summer and brought me back a small Eiffel Tower. It sat on my dresser for weeks and something about that sparked life in me again. Maybe it was the idea of going somewhere new or experiencing something different. In any case, by the end of that year, I knew I wanted to study business. And now I'm getting to study at one of the best business programs in the country.

I pull out my phone, hoping I'd have heard something from my brother today. It's been two days now since he's texted. I'm trying to give him space, but it freaks me out whenever he ghosts me.

As a twin, there's always a tug of connection with him and when I don't feel it, it fills me with a level of despair I can't shake. Especially knowing the state of mind he's been in since the accident.

A swatch of color grabs my attention from my peripheral vision and I catch a glimpse of someone walking into the classroom. The minute I lock eyes on the student, my chest tightens. Her hair is up in a bun, accentuating her perfect facial features and she's wearing a bright pink scarf that makes her big blue eyes seem even more blue. If I had the talent to paint the perfect woman, she would look just like this.

Of course it happens to be Kelsie. Why wouldn't she be here?

Kelsie stands for a moment in front of my table staring

at me. She rolls her eyes, tossing down her bag and then pins me with a glare. She jabs a painted fingernail toward me and mouths, "*Stay the fuck away from me, Hayes.*"

I give her a tight smile and a shrug, pointing out the futility of this request. "It's not like I planned this on purpose."

She grabs her stuff then whips back around sharply and moves up the steps toward the back section of the lecture hall before she takes a seat way up at the top. I internally groan. I figured we'd have classes together since we're in the same program, but I'd hoped it wouldn't be this awkward.

How am I ever supposed to apologize to her if she doesn't give me a chance?

A few other students trickle into the room, followed by a woman who looks to be in her mid-forties with her graying hair pulled back in a ponytail. She sets a bag on the table at the front of the lecture hall.

"Good morning, class, I'm Professor Wallen. This is Managing Family Business in an International Marketplace. So, if you're not here for that, you're likely lost, so scram."

This gets a few laughs and two very embarrassed students rush out of the room.

"I'll be going over the syllabus today and giving a brief introduction lecture. All of the materials should be on our class's webpage but if you'd prefer to have them texted or emailed, I can have my TA, Redding, do that. Let me know if you don't have access." She gestures toward a tall, skinny dude on the far wall toward the front. He gives a little wave and the prof continues. "Next class session, I'll be pairing each of you up for the main course project. I know everyone hates group projects, but there's no better way to learn how to operate and function out in the world than in teams or pairs."

The room lets out a collective groan and the professor chuckles.

"You'll have a paper and a presentation due at the end of the semester which will make up 75% of your overall grade. So, let's get started," she says cheerfully, turning on a computer as the screen projects at the front of the room.

I feel Kelsie's eyes boring into the back of my head, and I wait a few seconds before taking a surreptitious glance over my shoulder, but her eyes are on the screen.

I just hope to hell that we don't have any other courses together and no further awkward confrontations.

My last lecture of the day ends at four and I pack up my bag, hefting it over my shoulder with a sigh. Three new classes today and Kelsie happened to be in every single one of them. Fuck my life, this is going to be a long-ass semester. Especially if she continues with the silent treatment.

She hasn't spoken to me since our run-in this morning and it's killing me. I want to say something to her, but every time I get up the nerve, the professor shows up and I'm left feeling her eyes glued to me the entire lecture.

Or maybe that's just my guilt.

With a heavy sigh, I walk through the quad area that's sparsely filled with students and faculty heading home as I make my way to the gym for a team strength-training day.

As the kicker, I'm focused on leg workouts and drills. It's not exactly like kicking a soccer ball, but at least it's a familiar muscle memory for me. It's something tangible that

I can focus on instead of letting my mind wander where it shouldn't.

I check the map on my phone as I navigate across campus. I swear I'm getting a workout just trying to locate my classes. Fortunately the first two were in the same building, but that last one was on the other side of the quad.

When I arrive at the athletic facility, I find most of my teammates changing at their assigned lockers. I make quick work of putting on my gym clothes before heading into the weight room.

Killer is already on a leg machine and Hendy and EJ are lifting free weights. I glance at my phone to see if our strength and conditioning coach added anything to my training for today. I end up doing a lot more leg days than the average player because of my special team role. I warm up with several drills involving running in place and bringing my knees up high in a marching style and then low squats into high jumps. I finish with some balance stretching before heading over to weights.

Adding some weights to a bench press bar, I sit down at a bench.

"Hey, Killer, can you spot me when you got a sec?" I ask as I realize I may have added more weight than I should lift without a spotter.

"Fuck, yeah, dude. Let me just finish this rep," he grumbles. I watch him press out four more reps and then, with a clang, he finishes and walks over to me. He glances at the weights and nods his approval. I look up at his arms. Shit, this guy is stacked. He could probably bench press me.

He gets in position and I begin. "How was your first day?" he asks as he stands behind me.

"It was interesting," I mumble as I try for eight reps at this new weight.

"Interesting how?" he inquires as he leans forward a bit to look down at me.

"Kelsie was in every one of my classes," I huff as I feel my muscles tremble under the increased weight.

"Shit. That sucks. She must be really pissed at you. Hopefully she finds someone else to hook up with this semester and she'll forget about you. It's just hella awkward now. Grace and Lucy are like her best friends, which means...you know," Killer says with a sheepish grin.

"Dude, bros before hoes," Hendy yells over to us and we all chuckle.

EJ whacks him on the back of the head. "Shut the fuck up, Hendy. This isn't the nineties. We don't say shit like that anymore."

"We don't?" Hendy asks with a smirk.

EJ scoffs and throws a towel at him. "No...anyway, you always leave us for a woman. Never fails."

Hendy has the presence of mind to look contrite. "Well, they're prettier than you ugly bastards."

Killer glares at Hendy and then looks down at me. "Don't worry. We're teammates, man. We got your back. Now, our girls, on the other hand...well, just know they got their own friend code. So the sooner you can make nice with Kels, the better," he explains.

"Believe me, I'm trying," I mutter as I finish my third set.

Killer nods and then pauses. "Maybe pick her up some of the chocolate croissants at Madame Beaufort's on Second Avenue. It's this little French bakery and she fucking loves that shit. It could be like a peace offering or something."

I rub the sweat from my brow with the towel. "I'll have to try that. Thanks, Killer. Good suggestion."

He grins. "What can I say? I'm a wealth of female knowledge."

I chuckle and move to the leg press station.

One of the offensive tackles is over near Hendy and they chat, but I don't hear about what until Hendy yells out, "The Cougars are going down! I can't wait for our scrimmage!"

There's some hoots and hollers from different guys across the room and it reminds me why I'm here. I'm here because Kevin and Holden can't be and I need to focus on that. I can't let what's going on with Kelsie get in the way of my goal. As long as we can avoid each other at the house and act civil when we do come in contact, then maybe Killer is right, and she'll find someone else and lose this hatred she has toward me.

There's just one problem with that.

The mere thought of Kelsie with another man makes me crazy. I'd rather she just stay mad at me. If someone so much as touches her, I might lose my shit.

I'm not usually a jealous man, but what we had in Paris was special. We were so good together and then I fucked it all up.

I can only hope she'll let me explain why I had to do what I did. And when that time comes, she doesn't permanently close the door on us.

I shove my earbuds in my ears to drown out my teammates and contemplate how I can fix things between us.

I don't know if there's still a chance, but maybe I can try.

Just maybe, we can end up as friends.

Chapter Seven

K elsie

"Can you believe this shit?" I say through a mouthful of pretzel bites. "What a clusterfuck."

I finish chewing and dunk another pretzel bite into the beer cheese dip in front of me, shoving it into my mouth as I finish my rants over the recent turn of events with Hayes.

Lucy and Grace shake their heads and grimace over the news I've been whining about for the past ten minutes. The girls and I met up at The Brown Bear Cafe tonight for an early dinner before Lucy has to meet up with a new student she's tutoring at the library and Grace heads off to her computer geek club. It's our tradition to go out for dinner after our first day of classes and talk about our days.

I've kind of dominated today's conversation because the topic has been all about how Hayes is in every one of my classes and also happens to be my new housemate.

"That's the worst, Kels," Grace agrees, chomping on a nacho and picking at the long string of cheese that's stuck on her lip. "It just seems so obnoxiously crazy that he's everywhere you go."

"I know, right?" I growl, licking the cheesy goodness off my thumb.

Lucy, who's been her usual quiet and introspective self, pipes in. "You know, maybe it's the universe telling you something."

I narrow my eyes and give her a shut-the-fuck-up look. "Exactly what do you think it's telling me, oh wise one?"

She snorts. "Well...obviously there's some unfinished business that needs to be resolved between you two. You said so yourself that he's tried to explain what happened to you, but you've shut him down, right?"

I roll my eyes. "Yeah, because I don't give a good goddamn fuck what he has to say to me. What he did was unforgivable."

Grace and Lucy exchange glances and Grace heaves an exasperated sigh. I know what that means. I'm going to get a lecture.

"What?"

Gracie reaches a consoling hand across the table and places it over my knuckles.

"Kelsie, you know I love you...but staying angry with someone all the time will only eat you up inside. When you forgive that person, it opens your heart to new and wonderful things."

I scoff and make a gagging noise. "Thanks for your advice, Mother Teresa. How's that working out for you and your mom, huh?"

The pain that flashes over Grace's features makes me feel like a complete bitch. That was a low blow, even for me. She and her mother have had a difficult relationship ever since her parents got divorced years ago. She pulls her hand away and I snatch her wrist to tug her back.

"I'm an asshole, Gracie. I'm sorry. I didn't mean that. It's just been a shitty day and that was a shitty thing to say."

She blinks back the tears that threaten to spill over and nods. "I know. It's okay."

This whole thing with Hayes—from his unexpected arrival on campus, to the fact that he's everywhere I turn—has just made me so mad and turned me into a raving bitch. It's one thing to be angry with him, but now I'm taking it out on my best friends too.

"It's just that he's in my face at every pass and that asshat doesn't deserve my time or my forgiveness."

I know I'm digging my heels in on this one and being stubborn as fuck about letting it go, but goddamn it, he hurt me bad. I trusted him, he stole my heart, and he fucked me over. There's no coming back from that.

But mostly I'm angry with myself for falling for him so damn easily and seeing him everywhere reminds me of my stupidity. I've always been a casual hook-up girl with no strings attached. But when I met Hayes, I got too close, opened my heart, and then I got burned.

That will not happen again.

We continue eating our food as the waitress comes back to the table to ask if we want anything more. Although I'd love a beer to go with my pretzels, we order a few more sodas instead. Drinking and homework don't always mix.

We're just about finished up when a couple of guys walk through the entrance and by our table as they're seated.

One of them, Ben Hoffsteader from my Econ class, notices me as he passes the table and stops to say hi.

"Hey, Kelsie. How's it going?"

I wipe my mouth and smile brightly. Ben's a cute guy and we've hung out a few times at one of the frat houses.

He's a varsity hockey player who until recently was dating one of the cheerleaders. But word is they broke up because she was already talking marriage and babies, and he freaked out because that wasn't on his radar.

So now he's single and looking good enough to eat. Plus, if the rumors are true, he doesn't want to be serious with anyone right now. Just like me.

"Hey, Ben. It's good," I say, fluttering my eyelashes in that flirty way of mine. "Do you know my girls, Lucy and Grace?"

He nods his chin in greeting. "Hi, ladies. Nice to meet you. Didn't you go out with Hendy last year?"

Lucy's eyes grow wide at the mention of her one-time crush, Joel Henderson. But that's long in the past because she's been with her boyfriend Emmett since that time.

"Oh, yeah. We only went out a few times," she says with a blush. "I'm with Emmett Hudson now."

"Right on. He's good people." Then Ben returns his gaze back to me and his eyes flash with interest. "How about you, Kels? Are you seeing anyone?"

I give him a coy shoulder lift. "Why? Did you have someone in mind?"

He chuckles and shoves his hands in his front jeans' pockets. "I don't know. Maybe me...you should come to the game this weekend and we can meet up afterwards."

I hold out my hand. "Hmm...sounds interesting. Give me your phone and you can text me the deets. I might be able to fit that in my busy schedule."

Ben hands me his phone and I add in my digits under the name *Kelsie the Hot Chick*. When I give it back to him, he looks down and barks out in laughter. I grin at my outrageous confidence.

"You definitely are, Kels." He winks and then glances

over his shoulder at the table where his friends are already seated. "I better go. Nice meeting you guys. And, Kelsie, I'll text you later this week."

I wiggle my fingers at him in a wave goodbye as he turns and lumbers off toward his friends. Both girls stare at me like I have two heads.

"What?" I laugh, popping my last pretzel into my mouth, chewing and swallowing it down. "Seems to me that the best way to get over a guy is to find another one who's better."

Lucy giggles and rolls her eyes. "You can't argue with that logic. And that guy is one very tall and hot hockey player."

"I know, right?" I gaze in his direction and admire Ben's tall frame, his disheveled sandy-blond hair, and his bright blue eyes. "I heard hockey players really know how to handle their sticks too."

Yes, he is definitely not hard on the eyes.

But he's not the guy you fell in love with.

I push that errant thought from my head and take a giant sip of my diet soda through the straw.

"It's a bummer he's a hockey player and not on the football team, though," Grace laments, picking up one of her curly fries. "It would be cool if all three of us were dating guys from the same team."

I grouse at her idealism. "Nope, not gonna happen. I will never date a football player."

* * *

Over the next few days, I'm able to successfully avoid Hayes in the house by leaving a little later for my morning classes. We almost had a run-in this morning as I was closing my bedroom door. I heard him talking on the phone with someone as he was coming down the stairs. I assume it was his brother, Holden.

Since we agreed in Paris not to share anything too personal, I don't know much about his family or where he lives. But I do know about his identical twin, Holden.

God, one McIntyre guy is hard enough to bear...but two as hot and handsome as Hayes? I think I'd faint.

When I heard Hayes's voice, I ducked back into my bedroom to keep him from seeing me, but I could still hear a bit of what he was saying. It was weird because Hayes sounded so serious. Maybe even worried?

That's very un-Hayes-like. He's such an easygoing guy and always found a way to add levity and fun when we were together.

Now I shake those thoughts off, closing my laptop on my desk in the rear of the room and flicking my eyes to the back of Hayes's head. Then I remind myself that *I. Do. Not. Care.*

Professor Wallen finishes her lecture on today's topic. "Next class, we'll continue discussing the ways business owners assess the impact of the macroeconomic, political, and social indicators when making international business decisions." She closes her laptop and turns off the projector, the screen going dark at the front. Then she moves around the front and reaches for a sheet of printed paper on her desk. She slips on her reading glasses and leans against the desk.

"As I promised you during our first class, we're pairing you up with another student to work on your semester project. Redding and I reviewed the class roster and we have the final pair groupings. After I read them off, it's your responsibility to meet with your partner and review the project together. Barring any medical leaves of absence or other serious issues, these pairs are locked in and cannot be changed."

The girl sitting next to me, Molly, whom I met on Monday, leans over and whispers in my ear.

"I hope I get paired with that guy down in front," she nods her chin in Hayes's direction. "He is so cute. He looks like Jacob Elordi and Timothee Chalamet rolled into one tall man of deliciousness. And that hair...so yummy."

I cough and she gives me a strange look. "Uh, yeah. I guess."

The professor glances up in our direction with a look that says *I'm talking here*, and I swallow down any further comments.

She reads a few names from the first groupings and Molly's dreams are dashed when she's paired with a girl named Dominique. And then she reads off my name and I straighten my shoulders.

"Kelsie Dannon, you will be paired with..." She adjusts her glasses on the bridge of her nose and the anticipation is killing me.

Please don't be Hayes. Please don't be Hayes. Please don't be...

"Hayes McIntyre."

I wish the Universe would shut the fuck up already.

Chapter Eight

Hayes

The horror on Kelsie's face when Professor Wallen announced us as a pair is forever engraved in my brain. I'd swiveled around in my chair and caught a glimpse of her bitter contempt and then slunk back in my chair.

Great. Just great.

The way she's made herself scarce all week, I can't help but think she's avoiding me. And it doesn't help that I'm already swamped with training and my class schedule, so I haven't had time to approach her about the elephant in the room.

But at the moment, we're both home and she may be hiding in her bedroom because she knows it. I've been taking my time making myself a snack in the kitchen for the last ten minutes while secretly plotting a way to start a conversation with her. She's eventually going to have to speak with me since we've been paired up on the project we're assigned to work on together.

I'm about to make my move and go down to knock on her bedroom door when the doorbell rings. Frowning at the interruption, I set my bowl of chips down on the table and walk to the front door and answer it.

Standing out on the front porch is a guy I met at the football house a few weeks ago. I think his name is Ben and he's on the CFU hockey team. He seems like a nice enough dude from what I know of him.

"Oh, hey, Ben," I greet, standing in the entry, my hand on the doorframe, curious as to why he's here.

"Hey, man. I'm here for Kelsie. Is she ready?" he asks, looking around my shoulder into the front room and down the hallway behind me.

Ready? For what?

I'm about to ask him this question when suddenly Kelsie emerges from her room and walks up behind me. I get a whiff of her soft honey scent and something sizzles low in my gut.

I watch incredulously as she loops her hands around Ben's neck, lifts herself up on her tiptoes, and gives him a hug.

"Hi, Ben," she says and I can practically hear her smile. I fight a frown as she steps back and grabs her coat off the hook by the door.

Ben smiles, glancing at me with a lift of his brow before turning his gaze back to Kelsie. "You ready to go?"

What the hell? Where are they going? Is this like a date?

"Yep, sure am," she answers in a flirty voice that I heard a lot of in Paris. He steps in and takes the coat from her hands, helping her into it.

Oh, fuck no. He is not taking her *anywhere.*

I feel a sudden ragey hot anger radiate through my body and bubble up like I'm on fire from the inside out. I'm altogether uncomfortable, irritated, and severely confused about what is happening and I want to stomp around like an asshole and forbid her to go out with him. I want to yell *she's mine...* and then get down on my knees and beg her not to leave.

But I can't do that because she's *not* mine. She may be my housemate and my new class partner, but I have no right to prevent her from dating Ben.

The conversation I had with Killian comes rushing again in my head, where he said it might be a good thing if she started seeing someone else. At the time, I agreed. In theory, it sounds great. But in reality?

It fucking sucks.

"Don't wait up," Ben says, flashing me a knowing smile and a wink. A motherfucking wink!

I've not wanted to punch someone in a long time, but right now I want to beat the hell out of fucking hockey-playing Ben.

This feeling is completely irrational and not who I am at all. I know that, but I don't care. And when he places his hand on the small of Kelsie's back and guides her out the door, I see red and almost tackle his ass to the ground.

Kelsie turns her head and her eyes find me, her expression cold and calculating before she quickly steps through the threshold and Ben closes the door behind him. I stand there like an idiot, staring blankly after them through the front window.

For a moment, I wonder if I should run out after them or just go pound the shit out of a boxing bag at the gym?

When the hell did she start dating a hockey player? How did she get over me so fast?

All these questions roam through my head as I take deep breaths to calm my blood pressure. Minutes—or maybe hours—go by and I'm left with the realization that I'm still not over Kelsie and the feelings very much still linger there and haven't diminished in the least.

But I'll be damned if another man, no matter how nice of a guy he is, is going to touch my girl.

* * *

In the five hours that Kelsie was gone, I put a plan in motion to pull out all the stops to win her back. Or at the very least, get her to talk to me again. One step at a time.

Based on Killian's brilliant suggestion, I did some research and found a French bakery in a nearby town that appears to be owned by a French chef.

First step in Operation Get Kelsie to Talk to Me is getting her favorite pastries.

While Kelsie and our other housemates are still asleep this morning, I ordered half a dozen chocolate croissants and two cups of cafe au lait that arrive at 7:30 and I quietly bring it inside into the kitchen, eager for her to wake up.

Based on what I've heard each morning this week, Kelsie normally gets up around 7:45 to shower and get ready for her classes. So I sit and wait at the kitchen table, pretending to read an assignment, when all I'm really doing is listening for her to come in. Finally, I hear her bedroom door creak open and her feet padding down the hallway.

I take a deep breath and close my eyes, hoping like hell my plan works.

My head pops up from the book I've been reading and I watch as she strides into the kitchen and stops short when she sees me sitting here. She has on a very tiny pair of sleep shorts and a tank top. *Fuck.* I can see the entire outline of her breasts and her nipples pressed against the thin fabric. I quickly move my focus to her face.

I can't help but smirk when I see my plan is working as her gaze moves to the plate of pastries on the table. Her eyes close briefly as she inhales the scent of chocolate.

Bingo. I knew these would serve me well as a peace offering.

"Good morning," I offer with a quiet hopefulness. "I got us some breakfast from this French bakery over in Mountain Springs Killian told me about. I hoped we could chat a little about the project we were assigned."

I watch her eye the pastries and coffee dubiously, an eager pang flipping in my stomach.

She swallows and, after a few seconds, meets my gaze "What do you have in mind?"

Thank God! She's finally talking to me. I push the still warm *cafe au lait* over to her and she bites down on her lower lip before hesitantly taking the cup.

"When I was looking for a bakery, I found that the same family also owns a cheese company. They have headquarters near Paris; a store in Toulouse, France; and another store in Normandy, France and this small shop in Mountain Springs. I think they'd be perfect to interview for the assignment."

She quietly sips on her coffee and I tap my leg nervously waiting for her response.

"Yeah, sure. Okay. I have time today before our two o'clock class. Maybe you should call them and make sure they have time to meet with us?" she suggests, grabbing a croissant from the box and taking a bite. She moans at the deliciousness and closes her eyes, the sound resonating all the way to my dick.

"Oh, yeah, I can do that, but it's pretty short notice," I point out and grab my phone from the table to search their number for the Mountain Springs location.

"I know, but our first assignment for the project is due in two weeks," she points out, as if I'm not familiar with our timeline. "We don't have much time."

The phone rings twice and a woman with a French accent answers on the second ring. I quickly explain our situation as Kelsie keeps her eyes on me, her mouth and throat working as she continues to eat the flaky pastry. I feel my heart thumping in my chest because having her stand so close has me mesmerized, but also a bit nervous when I realize that we'll have to drive to get there. Although Mountain Springs isn't too far from the CFU campus, it will require a lot of highway driving, which makes me anxious after the accident. I don't do well when I'm driving long distances.

After finalizing the plans with the woman who was very eager to help us, I hang up and give Kelsie a winning smile and a thumbs up gesture.

"So the manager, Mallorie, said she could meet with us and give us a quick tour at three. From there we can schedule additional meetings as needed."

"Cool," she says appreciatively, licking the last remnants of her pastry from her lips. "I'll see you back here at 2:15."

I adjust myself under the table as I watch her tongue dart out again, remembering exactly what that tongue feels like when it slides up my cock.

"Holy hell, those are really good," she says as she plucks another croissant from the box and turns with her coffee and pastry, heading back to her room.

Well, it wasn't exactly a thank you, but at least we spoke. It's a start.

* * *

I buckle myself in the passenger side of Kelsie's car and inhale deeply, letting it go slowly as I count backwards from ten, trying to keep my nerves in check. Kelsie starts the engine, completely unaware of my anxiousness.

Her car is small, way too small, and the confinement has my heart beating fast.

When Kelsie offered to drive us, I didn't think much about it. I was just mentally preparing myself for riding in a car, period. I have to do it every time since my accident, regardless of who's driving.

Kelsie steers us onto the highway and reaches over to turn on some music, shuffling through the stations casually until she finds a song she likes and begins humming. I grip the door handle tight in my right fist and fiddle with the belt over my chest with my other hand.

My heart mimics the beat of the song in a fast, thumping rhythm. Sweat begins to dot my forehead and drip down my neck and my breathing becomes stilted. Shit, this was a bad idea. Such a bad idea. What was I thinking?

Every muscle in my body clenches, and my eyesight narrows into tunnel vision. I blink rapidly and drop my chin to my chest.

"Hayes, are you okay?" I hear Kelsie say, but her voice sounds like it's so far away.

Suddenly, the car slows down as she pulls over to the side of the road. Kelsie reaches a hand out, placing it over my forearm.

"Hayes?" she says softly. "Breathe, Hayes."

I take a deep breath and realize I've been holding it in as if I were drowning and couldn't breathe. My body begins to loosen and relax with each exhalation of air.

"Hey, look at me," she says, her voice laced with concern. Her small hand comes to my face and she takes my chin in her fingers and thumb to slowly turn my head toward her.

"What's happening right now?" she asks, searching my face for answers. "You are not okay. And I know I'm not that bad of a driver."

I lift my head and look at her, having almost forgotten how gorgeous her eyes are. The bright blue has softened into a muted hue, like the evening sky on a summer night. I chuckle at her attempt to lighten the mood and it distracts me long enough to allow me to find the words I need to speak.

"I...was in a bad car accident," I explain. "A few years ago."

She frowns. "Oh, no. I'm sorry. Were you hurt? Are you okay?"

I shrug. "Physically? Yes. Mentally, apparently not so much."

She nods and drops her hand. I immediately miss her touch on my face, but she keeps her other hand resting lightly on my forearm. It's the only thing anchoring me right now.

"Do you...always freak out in cars like this?" she asks as she looks down at where her hand touches my arm. "I don't remember it happening when we were together in Paris."

I shake my head. "No, I mean, we mostly took short rides in Paris or the subway, so it was okay. But highways, interstates...small two-lane country roads are tough. Sometimes I can psych myself up, but sometimes...I can't."

She squeezes my arm. "Was it a really bad accident?"

I normally hate it when people ask me about it and I seldom talk about it. It's still too hard. Too painful. Everything is still raw for me.

"Yes. It was bad," I manage to mutter through gritted teeth.

Kelsie's quiet for a moment, chewing on her bottom lip and memories of all the times I nipped that lip whirl around in my head. What I wouldn't give to kiss those lips right now. To use it as an escape from this humiliating car ride.

"I'm sorry you're still dealing with this, Hayes. You don't have to talk about it if you don't want to. But, um, should we continue on or..." She trails off as she looks at the road in front of us and then back to me.

I glance at her navi screen seeing that we're only two more exits from our turn. "Let's just go. We're only on this road for like three more minutes," I say.

"Are you sure?"

I nod. Hell no, I'm not sure, but we have to do this in order to get to our interview. I need good grades for my scholarship. There's too much riding on it and I can't fail.

"I'm going to hold your hand. If you need me to stop, just squeeze it, okay?" she says as she puts the car in drive and takes my hand in hers.

"Okay," I whisper.

She pulls out on the road and starts driving again. Something about her touch calms me and we make it to the second exit. I relax as soon as we get on a side street.

"We'll take a shortcut," she states.

I just nod, keeping my focus on the road ahead of us. Her hand squeezes mine and I rub my thumb over hers in a silent 'thank you' to her. I'm aware she wants to know more. And, shit, I want to tell her more.

The problem with opening up is it brings back painful memories and a flood of guilt. There's so much I want to tell Kelsie, and have since I left her hat night in Paris. It's all related and I'm a fucking mess.

I just hope that she'll give me a chance to tell her when I'm in a better state of mind. She deserves the truth...she deserves so much more than that.

Chapter Nine

K elsie

I've never seen Hayes flip out like the way he did in my car on the way to Mountain Springs.

He was clearly suffering from a panic attack, judging by the way his face turned a grayish-white, his pupils unfocused, and the clammy skin I felt when holding his hand. Every time he took a breath, it sounded like he was an asthmatic long-distance runner. I was worried he'd pass out while I was driving so I pulled the car over to make sure he was all right.

When he told me about the reason behind his episode, I was stunned. I had no idea he'd been in a bad car accident. He never once mentioned it when we were together in France. All the time we spent in each other's company and not a word. But I suppose that was par for the course, since we didn't divulge any personal details about our lives back home,

You never told him about your brother either.

Obviously, he's tried burying it all inside, but just like any trauma, it finds a way to bubble back up to the surface when he's faced with triggering events. Like riding in a car for a long distance.

He seemed to be much calmer on our way home, but I also made sure to drive like a grandma, staying under the speed limit and avoiding any quick stops and starts, even when my instinct is to drive fast. I even held his hand again for most of the trip back, as uncomfortable as it was for me.

I don't want to touch him. I don't want to get close to him. I don't want to make the same mistake twice.

The best course of action is to steer clear of Hayes. But that doesn't seem to be an option because the universe is doing its best to pull me back into Hayes's orbit. I want so badly to stay mad at him and not forgive him for breaking my heart, but then he goes and does sweet things for me.

Like this morning when he went out of his way to find the French bakery to get me breakfast and also found the topic of our project.

I guess I should give credit where credit's due.

The initial interview with Mallorie at the Toulouse Cheese Company of Mountain Springs went really well. She was so kind and generous, and provided us with some great material for us to get started. Now we need to combine our notes and create our thesis and an outline for our project.

When we got back into the house, I'd immediately gone into my bedroom to change into my comfy clothes and read the texts that had come in while I was driving.

The first one was from Lucy on our group chat.

Lucy: Hope you made it home safe and had a good trip. We want to hear all about it.

Lucy: We're having pizza tonight if you want to come over.

Grace: You better come over and tell us what happened! And how did your date with Ben go?

Lucy: We need all the deets, girly!

I laugh at the exchange and shoot a quick message back.

Me: The interview went great. Still need to work on some notes. I'll come over later.

I'm contemplating what I want to tell them about my date last night with Ben. It gave me such satisfaction to walk out of my bedroom, looking fine as fuck, to prove to Hayes that I was over him and have moved on.

But that feeling was short-lived when I saw the look on Hayes's face. It was a cross between jealousy and torture. Truthfully, it kind of soured my mood for the rest of the night and I wasn't exactly in the best frame of mind while out with Ben.

Speaking of which, I also have another text from him I should respond to.

Hottie Hockey Player: Hey, Kels. Our home game's tomorrow night. You coming? Party afterwards at Delta Chi.

Hottie Hockey Player: I'd really love to see you.

I inhale deeply and let it out.

Gah. Ben. What do I do with him? Yes, I like him. He's really hot and proved to be a good kisser. But something's missing and I didn't feel the same *umph* of chemistry like I do with Hayes.

Correction. Like I *did* with Hayes.

I thought accepting the date with Ben would be a good way to get back to my normal self, where I could just have a casual hookup with a guy who wasn't looking for anything serious.

I'd hoped hanging out with Ben would help me forget about Hayes. Instead, Ben is starting to bug me.

Throughout the day, while I was in classes and then with Hayes in Mountain Springs, Ben texted me at least a dozen times. Maybe some other women like that, but not me. It feels smothering. Too needy.

Hayes was never like that when we were together.

In the four months we dated in Paris, he was so good about giving me the space I needed to do my art and hang out with my friends. He didn't constantly pester me or text me when we were apart.

The knock on my door startles me and I leave the text unanswered as the phone slips from my hand and drops to the floor. I spin around to see Hayes standing on the other side of my open doorway.

"Sorry, Kels. I didn't mean to scare you," he says with a contrite smile and then hooks his thumb down the hallway. "I was just gonna let you know I'm ready when you are."

I bend down to pick up my phone and nod. "Yep, I'm ready. Was just checking my messages."

He lifts a brow with interest and coughs. "Any more from the hockey player?"

Yeah. Too many.

But I kind of like that it might make him jealous that I went out with Ben. I know he saw the stream of incoming texts from Ben while I was driving because they'd pop up on the display in my phone holder.

Part of me wants to tell Hayes it's none of his business. On the other hand, though, I might just use this as an opportunity for some payback.

"As a matter of fact, yes. A few were from Ben." I flip off the light switch and scoot around Hayes, catching a whiff of his clean ocean breeze and spice scent. I can feel his eyes on my ass as I walk in front of him toward the main living area. I swing my head over my shoulder and catch him staring at me, but he quickly diverts his gaze and I grin. "We had fun last night and he asked me to come watch his game tomorrow night."

"Oh...well, that's cool."

We settle in on the couch in the living room since Eleanor is in the kitchen making dinner.

I call out to her as I tuck my feet under my butt on the couch. "Whatever you're making in there sure smells good."

Eleanor is a grad student from Texas and is studying anthropology. From the sounds of her giggles, her boyfriend, Martin, is also in there with her.

Eleanor pops her head around the corner wearing a gap-toothed smile and a grease-stained apron. "I'm missing home so I'm showing Martin how to make my grandma's southern fried chicken and dumpling recipe."

"She lies!" Martin shouts back in a teasing tone. "It's just an excuse to get me to cook for her and to boss me around."

"You love it when I'm bossy, don't you, baby?" Eleanor purrs in a southern drawl.

I bite my lip and lock eyes with Hayes, smiling in his

spot on the couch next to me. We both laugh at the couple's super cute banter.

Hayes and I were hopelessly lovesick like that too at one point. But that ended when he fucked me over.

Eleanor continues, "And let me remind you that when we get married, I will *not* be the only one cooking."

My eyes grow wide because this is news to me. I haven't heard about this. "Wait, what? Did you two just get engaged?"

Martin snorts from the kitchen. "Not yet. This fiercely independent woman keeps rejecting my proposals. I'd hoped cooking for her would do the trick."

We hear a clatter of pans and then an *"Oof"* as I stifle my laughter with my hand over my mouth.

When I look at Hayes, he shakes his head in mirth and rolls his eyes. I reach out to smack his arm playfully and then snatch it back, remembering I'm not supposed to touch him.

"What do you know about it?" I scoff.

"Oh, trust me," he says, raising a brow at me.

Quickly turning away, I pick up my notebook on the table in front of us to focus my attention on anything but his face.

"I know a thing or two about fiercely independent women. One in particular."

Hayes pokes me in the thigh with his finger and I jerk my leg away. I don't want him touching me either.

We may have to spend a lot of time together due to this project, but I do not have to like it. And I don't want to like him.

"Don't know what you're talking about," I murmur, flipping through the pages to find a blank one to begin our project. "Okay, where shall we start?"

Chapter Ten

Hayes

After two hours of working on our project outline, I'm exhausted, hungry, frustrated, and buzzing with need.

I thought I could manage my feelings and my physical reactions to being around Kelsie, but it's fucking hard.

Between the stress of the car ride and the incessant text messages she keeps getting from Ben, I'm about to lose my shit.

"Kelsie, can you please just concentrate? Enough with the texting already," I growl out in exasperation.

I swear her phone has been pinging every second in the past few hours. Each time it does, my body vibrates with a need for a release I don't know how to get.

"I am," she snaps back, glaring at me from behind her phone. "I can't help it that everyone wants me right now."

I scowl. "Your booty call can fucking wait."

I try to tap out my last thought into the shared document we've been working on but feel her eyes boring into me. If she could shoot lasers from them, I'm pretty sure I'd be dead right now. I steal a glance at her from my peripheral vision and notice her body appears wound as tight as mine.

"He is not a booty call," she snarls back. "And what do you care?"

"I don't," I reply testily.

God, why am I acting like this? It feels like we are on some emotional roller coaster today and my stomach is tangled in knots.

"You know what?" She slams her laptop closed and stands, folding her arms over her chest.

I make the bad decision to look up and see the way her boobs are pushed up between her elbows.

I leisurely put my feet on the coffee table because I'm not going anywhere. Not until I finish this damn outline that's due later this week "What?"

"ARGH! You are so frustrating!" she says loudly, kicking my feet off the table. I press my lips together to keep from laughing. She's acting like a petulant child.

"Yeah, well so are you, Kelsie. But we need to finish this outline...so do you think we can do that?" I ask, deciding to take the high road. One of us has to be an adult for a moment.

She sits back down in a chair with a huff and opens her laptop again while continuing to glare at me. "Fine."

We spend another thirty minutes hashing out details and trying to get our outline into a better format. It's way more time than I wanted to devote to this exercise. And as we work, it's like Kelsie is trying to taunt and tease me, turning me into a frustrated, horny dude.

Earlier, she changed into a tank top with a low cut neckline and no bra. Her shorts—if you can call them that—are those tight black booty shorts that cling to her thighs. I sneak a peek as she moves her legs, pressing her heels under her ass. Is she even wearing underwear?

Every time she takes a breath, her perfect tits rise and fall. Fuck me. I remember when I fucked those perfect tits. I have done unspeakable things to those breasts and the image of them is seared into my brain.

"Stop staring at me," she murmurs over her laptop screen as she moves a section of our outline. I watch her highlight the text on my screen and then she does the one thing that gets me every time.

I watch as she outlines her bottom lip with her thumb, then draws it down over her chin, over the expanse of her neck until it stops right in the pocket of her cleavage. Does she really want to play this game?

Fine. Game on.

"It's getting hot in here," I state and, without a second thought, whip my t-shirt off and toss it next to my bag on the floor. I lean back into the sofa cushions, letting my gray sweatpants fall further down my hips. She used to love my abs and obliques and would trace them with her fingers endlessly as we lay in bed together. I steal another glance and find her eyes glued to my abdominals.

I smirk.

"Yeah, it is kind of hot now that you mention it," she agrees, taking the hem of her tank top and tugging it up past her belly button and then tying a knot between her breasts. I glance at her stomach.

Goddamn, she is so hot. I remember running the tip of my tongue around the center of her belly button before I'd move south to the waistband of her panties.

My cock begins to thicken in my sweats and I know if she looks, she'll see the very visible outline of my hard-on. I do my best to focus on this last section of our outline, but it's useless.

Her phone pings again and it takes every fiber of my being not to grab it and chuck it against the wall. It's like she's doing this on purpose to get me riled up.

Earlier today, she was so kind. She could have been obnoxious about my panic attack in the car, but instead she pulled over and gave me a glimpse of the Kelsie I once knew. Now, she's acting like a total pain in my ass. I think she's getting pleasure out of dangling herself in front of me as if I'm a kid and she's the candy on a top shelf that I can't reach, candy I've had before, candy that I know tastes amazing.

I watch her respond to a text and I ball my hands into fists.

"We should talk," I say out of nowhere, pushing my laptop off my lap and then realizing my mistake when she lifts her gaze and it lands on my crotch.

"About what?" she asks, tilting her head to the side and smirking. "The fact that you get turned on while working on an outline about international business practices?"

I glance down at my sweatpants and unabashedly adjust my cock. "No, not that. We have...unresolved...things to discuss, don't you think?"

She sighs. "Don't want to hear your excuses. And besides, I think I'm going to grab a late night snack with Ben. So, let's wrap this up."

She closes her laptop and stands, heading toward her bedroom.

"Kelsie, wait," I call out, hoping she'll listen and give me a chance.

She waves me off and then turns the corner, shutting me

out quite literally. What the fuck? I want to go after her. I want to make her listen to what I have to say.

I need to explain myself. She deserves to hear the truth, if I can just spit it out. I almost explained it when she pulled the car over earlier today. I wanted to, but I was in a full-blown panic attack. When I get like that, I can't think straight and I'll need to have my wits about me when I tell her everything.

If I tell her everything about the accident. Because if she knew all of it, she'd hate me even more than she does now. Who wouldn't? Guilt wraps around my heart and squeezes it like a vise. As if on cue, my phone pings with a text.

Holden: How's that project going?

I had told him about my project when he finally got in touch with me and that I was paired up with Kelsie. I didn't exactly explain everything because if he knew why she was mad at me, he'd feel bad about it.

I'm not sure who harbors more remorse; me or Holden. Most days it's a toss-up, but then I remember I can still live out his dream and he's still stuck in a rut at home. I punch the sofa cushion with my fist. Life is not fair. None of this is fair.

I take a deep breath, trying to calm myself down.

Me: It's going. Today was all right. We at least got the first draft of the outline done.

Holden: That's good. Hope you work things out with her.

Me: Yeah…we'll see.

God, this sucks. I wish Kevin was here. If he was, he'd totally know what to do. He was my best friend and there are days I need him more than anything. I just need someone to talk to.

Even though Holden's my twin, I can't always share everything with him. He's still too fragile, so if I mention anything that isn't positive, I feel like it'll send him in a downward spiral.

I don't know my teammates well enough to really share anything with them. And the only other person in my life I'd like to talk to...is currently pissed off at me and about to go out on a date with another guy.

That about sums up my life.

I hear the door to Kelsie's room open and then she appears in the hallway and my jaw drops open.

She's changed into a snug-fitting crop top in hot pink accentuating her tight abdominals. The black leggings hug her perfect ass and the bra underneath the top pushes up her tits in the most tantalizing way. It has me vibrating with the need to...well, do something.

Before I know what I'm doing, I stand abruptly and zero in on her like a launched missile heading toward the target.

She looks up from her phone, startled that I'm suddenly so close.

Her mouth opens to say something, but the words die on her tongue when I cage her between my arms, my palms flattening against the wall. A gasp escapes her lips.

"What are you doing?" she seethes through gritted teeth, but the look in her eyes tells me a different story. They flicker with heat and lust.

I lean down and growl, "Are you going out with him to make me jealous?"

She rolls her eyes and then snorts "It's none of your business why I'm going out with him."

I press in close so her breasts touch my chest. I feel every breath. Each inhalation and exhale. I lean my head down so my lips are at her ear.

"It is my business," I whisper, my breath fanning over her neck. Breathing in her warm honey scent, I nearly lose my goddamn mind.

"Not anymore."

"It never stopped being my business."

"Fuck you, Hayes!" she says in a harsh tone, shoving me away with her palm. "You have no right because you left. Not me. You." She digs a fingernail into my chest. While the pain is slight, her words cut deep.

"You're right, I did, but—"

"No! No buts! I hate you!" she shouts loudly.

I'm not sure if anyone else is upstairs in this house at the moment, but if they hear the shouting, they might wonder what's going on and jump in to intervene.

Kelsie tries to push me away, her phone slipping from her hand and clattering to the floor. But she pauses, casting a glance at the phone and then back to me.

Instead of pushing me away, her hands move to my hips and she grips the hem of my waistband. I feel the electricity between us as the air seems to shift and I suck in a sharp breath. Her pupils dilate.

Wait. What just happened here?

"You want me, don't you?"

"No," she replies unconvincingly, fingernails digging into my skin at my waist. "As if..."

I run a single finger over the curve of her collarbone and then down her cleavage. Her breasts heave with a shuddering inhale of breath.

"Yes, you do," I urge as I trail a finger around her nipple that hardens under my touch.

She sucks in another breath and repeats her mantra, this time with far less force and conviction. "Fuck you, Hayes. I hate you."

"You already said that," I tease and then shiver when I feel her finger trace over the ridges of my obliques.

"I do...hate you. I don't want you," she murmurs and glances down at the bulge in my sweatpants. She bites down on her bottom lip and she avoids my gaze.

I lean down, inhaling more of her delectable scent and run my nose along her neck.

"Then prove it."

Chapter Eleven

Kelsie

I'm at war with every instinct in my body.

My brain tells me to leave, to walk away and not touch him.

But every cell. Every molecule. Every part of my being wants to hate fuck him right now. To let him fuck me against this wall so hard it will shake him free from my memories and get him out of my system once and for all.

I close my eyes tightly, trying to shut out the arousal that churns and twists through my bloodstream like a goddamn hurricane.

I remind myself why fucking him would be a bad idea.

Even though it would feel so, *so* good.

Every moment I've spent in Hayes's company today has increased the level of desire that lives in me like an electric live wire, super-charged and amped, ready to spark with one touch from him.

As Hayes presses in closer, his arms crooked at my sides to block me in, my nipples harden and poke against my tank and my chest heaves against his bare torso.

Jesus H. Christ. How am I supposed to resist him when he's this close to me in this state of undress?

I keep my fingers locked in position at the waistband of his sweats, but they itch to roam over the heat of his body. He's still shirtless and his broad shoulders and tempting muscular chest are too strong for me to resist. I lift my hand and flatten my palm against his pecs, the connection producing a sizzling sensation that shoots straight south and floods my panties.

I let out an aggravated grunt. I'm so turned on and angry, and I don't know what to do with all these emotions. All I know is I have a raging need to crash my mouth against his and fucking kiss the hell out of him.

I shove my fingers through his tousled hair, lock my grip, and pull his mouth toward mine. Our lips crash together in a brutal collision of need, angst, and desire.

Hayes groans against my lips and I fist the ends of his hair tighter in my grasp. I'm not sure if it's meant to prod him to kiss me harder, or it's lashing out against this attraction.

All I know for certain is I might die if he doesn't get naked and fuck me right this instant.

I throw a leg around his waist and his hands curl underneath my ass, lifting my feet off the floor and pinning me against the wall. I wrap my other leg around his backside and dig my ankles into his lower back. When his hard erection wedges in place between my legs, we each let out a sigh of relief.

Our bodies now aligned, Hayes begins to thrust against me, grunting with every wild grind of his cock over my leggings. My panties are damp and the friction over my clit has me bearing down as he moves against me.

Yes, yes, yes. This is what I need.

"Fuck me, Hayes," I murmur between choppy breaths. Hayes pulls back and stares at me with a desire so strong I just might collapse from its impact.

Somewhere in the quiet of the house I hear footsteps coming down the stairs. One of our other roommates is on their way down to the kitchen. Although we are relatively hidden against the wall and are out of view from anyone, it's not absolutely private either.

Hayes spins us around and walks down the hall to my bedroom, kicking my door closed with his heel before dropping me on the bed.

"Take off your pants," he orders and my eyes flare at his command. I love this naughty side of Hayes. He unties his sweatpants and shoves them down his legs. My mouth dries as I gape at his hard cock springing free.

God, how I've missed that bad boy.

"Commando?" I say, raising a brow as I lift my ass and wiggle my leggings down to my feet before kicking them off.

Hayes quirks a smile and then drops to the floor in front of me, pressing his fingers into my inner thighs and spreading my legs wide.

His mouth is on me in a flash. With one swipe of his tongue, he licks a strip of my skin so close to where I want him, I tremor in response. He wastes no time with teasing kisses or touches.

This isn't about love or sweet flirtation.

This is down and dirty, get you out of my system, straight up hate fucking.

Pinching the seam of my panties, he shoves the cotton panel over to expose my core, and then zeroes in on my clit.

I cry out and squirm underneath the warmth of his mouth. He nips, sucks, and licks at my pussy, tonguing at my entrance as I hold on to my sheets for dear life.

"Fuck, Kels. I need to be inside you."

He says this as he thrusts two fingers inside my pussy and I spasm and cry out.

"Yes!"

The orgasm crashes through me without warning, hitting me with the intensity of an earthquake, shaking me to the core.

My breaths come out in labored pants as I flop back against the mattress. Closing my eyes, I hear a condom wrapper being ripped open. I'm not sure where it came from, but I don't care.

When I lift my head, I watch Hayes as he sheathes his cock, pulling it tight at the base before stroking it in his grip. When our eyes connect again, he smirks.

"You still hate me?"

"More than ever," I sputter out, trying to keep the smile off my face, and then gasp when he draws a thumb through my seam, using the wetness gathered there to lubricate his cock. Then he slams inside me and literally takes my breath away.

Memories come flashing back in a speedy torrent as Hayes sets a punishing rhythm, rocking his hips forward and back. I remember the first time we fucked inside my Paris flat, knowing instantly that the connection we shared was too big for just a one-night stand. I worked so hard to guard my heart, but somehow Hayes knew the code. He had the key all along.

I'd hoped he lost it after he left me in Paris.

Emotions swirl like tide pools inside my head as I valiantly try to block them out. I focus on the sensations that build between my legs. With each thrust of his pelvis, Hayes brings me closer and closer to the edge again.

"Fuck, Kels," he murmurs, grinding and tilting his hips

to drive harder and faster. "You going to be a good girl and come again?"

"Fuck you, Hayes. I'm *not* your girl."

He chuckles and leans down to bite my shoulder.

That motherfucker. I'll show him.

I snag my hands behind him and dig my fingernails into his skin, dragging them sharply down his back. The growl it produces from his chest has me trembling in pleasure so I do it again.

"You filthy little brat," he sneers before he crushes his mouth over mine for a possessively dirty kiss. I suck on his tongue and he bites at my lower lip.

I come in a rush of climatic sparks, shooting into the cosmos like a runaway star. My heels dig into his calves and he grunts in either pleasure or pain, I'm not sure which.

"So. Fucking. Good," Hayes mutters out before dropping his head into my neck and, with three more pumps of his hips, he releases inside me. I can feel his dick pulsing against my inner walls and I clench in response.

Finally, Hayes lets out a long breath and pulls out, rolling to his side next to me.

We lay there for a few moments, silence descending upon us, bringing us back to reality.

If that wasn't enough, my phone rings from somewhere down the hallway where I dropped it during our heated kiss.

"Oh, shit," I sputter, remembering I'm supposed to be meeting Ben at the bar. I jump out of bed to search for my panties. When I locate them, I bend over to slip them on just as Hayes encircles my wrist with his fingers. I snap my head to stare at him.

"Don't go, Kels. Stay with me."

He's propped himself up on an elbow, his dark hair

hanging loosely at his shoulders. When we were back in Paris, he'd told me he was going to have it cut before he started school again. But he didn't. It's longer now than when we first met at the sidewalk café. His dark hair and long eyelashes are what drew me to him in the first place.

But now...they only remind me of the hurt he caused me and I don't want to feel that way.

I shake his hand free and continue to get dressed, ignoring his request for me not to leave.

Maybe a part of me wants to stay here. But the other part—the one that still wants to exact my revenge and get even with him—wants to show him I don't need him anymore. I have another guy who is interested and won't hurt me because I won't ever let another guy that close to my heart again.

"I'm late. This was a mistake." I adjust my shirt, tugging it over my breasts and then fluffing my hair with a slide of my fingers through the strands. "It's a one and done, Hayes. Nothing's changed."

He springs up and sits on the edge of my bed. I avoid his eyes because I don't want to see what's there.

A sigh leaves his lips. "Yes, it has and you know it."

Spinning on my heels, I point a finger at him. "Don't tell me what I do or don't know, Hayes. The only thing I know right now is that I'm late for my *date* with *Ben*."

He scoffs. "So you're just gonna fuck me and then run off and fuck him too, Kels? Is this all a game to you?"

His eyes flash with pain and for a second I feel a wave of guilt wash over me.

But then the moment is gone. Hayes stands up, rips off the used condom, and throws it in my trash with an angry bark of laughter. He bends down to slide on his discarded sweats and stalks off toward the door.

When he turns back to face me, his expression has changed. It's morphed into something like resigned anguish.

"You are the most aggravating woman I've ever known, you know that?"

I cross my arms over my chest. "And you're the worst. I guess we're even."

In two strides, he's backed me into a wall again, slapping one hand above my head to hover over me.

"You say that, Kels, but I know the truth. You're using that guy because he's safe."

I scoff and roll my eyes. "Safe? He's a 200-pound hockey player. How is that safe?"

Hayes bends down and pins me with his eyes. "He's safe because he's not me."

"Thank God for that."

The words come rushing from my mouth and I push him away, turning around to stomp out of my room. I snatch up the phone from the hallway floor, grab my jacket, and walk out the front door.

How the hell did things get so screwed up?

And how much longer can I last before I admit that he's right?

Chapter Twelve

Hayes

And just like that, we're right back at square one.

Kelsie sits on the far side of our lecture hall avoiding me like the plague, and I'm too exhausted from my early morning training to deal with our current situation.

I stayed up all night stewing over what happened. The amazing sex we had, followed by the way she just left to be with "what's-his-name," drove me crazy with jealousy and resentment.

The professor yammers on about some process for marketing as I sit slumped in my chair, my baseball cap pulled low to cover my face. I'm partially listening while sneaking glances at Kelsie every few minutes. She's sitting down closer to the door today, giving me a good view of her profile.

She never once looks my way, but that doesn't keep me from replaying that hot-as-hell hate sex scene we had yesterday over and over in my head like some sort of bad reality show I can't stop watching. I can't forget the way she squirmed when my tongue brought her to orgasm or how her tight pussy felt wrapped around my cock. It was like coming home. Everything about it felt right. Well, almost. At least the physical release.

We need to work on the other interpersonal stuff. If she would stop being such a stubborn pain in the ass and give me a chance to talk, I could try to explain things.

Try harder.

The professor finishes the lecture, but I'm so zoned out I don't realize it until one of the students accidentally kicks my foot when they pass my seat and I bolt upright. Shit, I hope this lecture material isn't going to be on a quiz tomorrow because I will fail.

I shove my laptop in my bag and glance over to see Kelsie already filing out of the lecture hall, swarmed by a couple of classmates who are looking for her attention. By the time I zip up my bag and exit the room into the hallway, she's disappeared.

I scan the corridor past the people lingering about or hurriedly walking to their classrooms but don't see her anywhere, so I head to the student union to grab a protein shake from the coffee stand.

While I wait to place my order, I see Hendy striding confidently into the building, bag slung over his shoulder, nodding to people as he goes. When he sees me, he nods with his chin and heads in my direction.

"What's up, Mac?" he says, clapping me on the back in a friendly gesture.

"Not much."

Everything. I'm a mess and fucked up with Kelsie *again* is what I really want to say.

Instead, I smile, give him a handshake and motion

toward the menu board behind the counter. "Just grabbing a smoothie before I head home to study."

"Fuck, yeah. I love their smoothies. Bear-y-licious is the best," he says jovially, and then turns his megawatt smile toward the cashier taking orders, who proceeds to blush profusely and beaming at him like he's a rock star.

Jesus. I wonder what it's like to be a guy like Joel. QB extraordinaire. Star football player. The one everyone always clamors to be around. Joel Henderson can't go anywhere on this campus without being recognized or fawned over. I would hate that kind of recognition, but he seems to enjoy the shit out of it.

I've never wanted to be that guy or have that kind of attention focused on me. Holden may have had aspirations of that at one point, but not me.

I step up to the counter to place my order and the girl smiles politely at me, but then her attention darts to Hendy and I swear she stares at him with fucking hearts in her eyes.

"Hey, Hendy," she coos, toying with the ends of her hair flirtatiously, promptly forgetting I'm even there.

He bends down and leans on his elbows over the counter, producing a cheeky grin.

"Hey, Bree," he drawls out in a low tone. "How you doing?"

She giggles and flutters her lashes. I clear my throat to get their attention and Hendy chuckles as the girl finally offers to take my order.

We move down to the end of the bar to wait for my drink, as Hendy leans casually against it, one foot propped over the other.

"Hey, it's movie night at the house if you want to come by tonight," he offers, scanning around the student lounge and acknowledging people as they walk by. I try to hide my grimace at the prospect of going through a similar scene that happened at their party a few weeks ago. The last thing I need is Grace and Lucy glaring daggers at me and wishing I were eaten by a fire-breathing dragon.

"Are you sure? I thought I was banned for life." The words spill out before I even register them. They aren't meant to be rude, just a confirmation. "Will the girls be there?"

Hendy chuckles, angling toward me conspiratorially. "Word is that you've been given the green light. I don't know what changed. Maybe it's because Kelsie is seeing that hockey player and her attention is elsewhere."

I scowl and inwardly groan. There's no way I could sit through a movie if Kelsie and Ben are fucking making out in front of me.

"I don't know. Next time, maybe. I really got to go over the stuff from class today. And since we have that spring scrimmage coming up, I need to work with the special teams coordinator out on the field," I offer, hoping it sounds plausible.

"Shit, you're a better student than me," he laughs congenially. "Well, if you decide otherwise, or maybe after your practice, feel free to stop over."

I nod with a smile. "Sure thing, bro. Thanks for the invite."

"Of course, dude. You're part of the team. You're always welcome," he says, grinning as his gaze shifts to a petite brunette on the other side of the student lounge. "Gotta run. See you later, Mac."

I nod and watch as he saunters over to the woman who seems to wear the same heart eyes expression as Bree the cashier. She gives him a hug. Damn, Hendy definitely has swagger.

As I take the walk through the quad and back to my off-campus house, I consider his invite. A part of me wants to go over tonight and chill with my new friends. I need some distraction from my overactive thoughts on Kelsie and the situation with my brother. By the time I get home, though, I decide against the movie night in order to study. I need to maintain my grades so I can keep my scholarship and spot on the team. Otherwise, this entire transfer will be for nothing.

I can always hang out another time.

It's not even past 4 p.m. when the winter dusk settles in and it's grown dark by the time I make it back home. As I turn the corner of the street, I happen to glance up at the old house from the front walkway. There's a light on in the attic dormer window. No one lives up there, to my knowledge as all our housemates have their own rooms. Although I've never been up there, I thought Parker mentioned it was just used for storage.

I enter the house, kick off my shoes by the door, and wave to Parker who sits with her back to me at the kitchen table, head bent over her laptop, fingers flying as she types what appears to be a paper.

"Hey," I say, hoping not to interrupt her. She doesn't look my way, but throws a hand in the air in greeting.

I haven't gotten to know Parker all that well yet. All I know is her father owns this house, she's lived here the last two years, and she hopes to go into broadcast journalism when she graduates.

Glancing down the hall toward Kelsie's room, I notice her door is shut and there's no light coming from inside.

Looks like she might be gone. I suppose that's a good thing since I have studies to do.

I take the flight of stairs up to my bedroom and toss my bag on the bed. But curiosity gets the better of me and I want to see why there's a light on from behind the attic door. I climb the narrow flight of stairs to the third floor.

Light streams down into the staircase and as I round the corner, Kelsie comes into view. She's standing with her back to me, wearing a pair of her paint-splattered overalls, a white tank top beneath, facing a large canvas propped up on an easel. She's barefoot even though it's cold as fuck up here. And she's...painting.

Quietly, I watch her for a long moment as she strokes the brush of light brown paint along the canvas. I didn't realize she was still painting, considering she told me it was just a hobby. I figured now that we're back in school, she wouldn't have time. But while in Paris, she showed me some of the artwork she'd completed because she was inspired.

When I mentioned how talented I thought she was and asked her why she wasn't studying art in college, she just shrugged me off and said she'd never make a living at it, so why bother?

Quietly and without detection, I make my way over to stand against the far wall, taking in her exquisite body and the graceful movements of her arm as she sweeps color across the canvas. Then she stops and puts the end of the brush between her teeth, tilting her head from side to side to assess what she's created. She plucks it from her lips, putting the brush back to the canvas and stroking another swath along the edge.

I've never seen anything as sexy as when Kelsie paints.

My eyes wander across the room where I notice several more paintings—some finished and others in a state of incompleteness—lined up against the attic floor. How many paintings has she done since she returned to school? I can't believe I didn't know she came up here.

But then again, there's a lot I don't know about Kelsie still.

"That's really good," I offer out of the blue, my voice echoing over the cold dusty floor.

The paintbrush clatters to the floor when she jumps and then spins around to clutch at her heart.

"Jesus H. Fucking Christ! Hayes, you scared the living shit out of me!"

I give her an apologetic smile as she bends down to pick up the fallen tool and then wipes off the smudge of paint it left over her boob.

When she turns to fully face me, I see she has paint smeared on her right cheek and left arm. She's a mess and so fucking adorable.

A perfect, beautiful mess with her hair piled in a high bun on top of her head, disheveled with strands of blonde popping out and falling over her face.

I take a few steps closer to get a better look at her work and she stops me by stepping in front of the canvas, blocking it from my view. I wrinkle my forehead with a frown over her reaction.

"It's not done yet," she murmurs, fluttering the hand in the air that still holds the paintbrush, uncertainty lacing her tone.

I peek around her, pointing at the art. "I've seen your stuff before, Kels. Your art is amazing."

A look of vulnerability passes through her eyes, which surprises me. Because Kelsie is anything but weak or unconfident. She's the fiercest woman I know and the brightest star in the sky.

She slowly steps aside. "Please don't judge it. I'm not done with it yet."

"I promise I won't."

What I see takes my breath away and I smile wistfully at the scene in front of me. It's a park in Paris near the Seine where we used to go for walks. Where we'd stroll along the path beside the bank of the river and later make out on a blanket while the world moved around us in slow motion. The painting floods my mind with my memories of us sitting there for hours talking, our hands entwined, or when she'd lie on my lap as I stroked her hair. Or times we'd be studying, books on our laps, and my arm would be wrapped around her shoulder. Then just for the hell of it, she'd turn her head and kiss me on the cheek. My heart constricts at those memories.

Those were the best days of my life.

The time I spent in Paris with her made me forget all about the pain I left behind in Colorado.

Her painting captures the beauty of our experience perfectly.

"I love it," I state matter of factly, feeling a little choked up.

"You do?" She twists her lips in question.

"I do. You have a talent for capturing a place exactly as it was with every detail colorfully represented. It's really good, Kelsie. I'm so glad you've found a place and some time to continue your work."

"Thanks."

She turns back around and starts to reorganize her supplies. I sigh.

"Kelsie, we need to talk about what happened."

She shakes her head. "No, we don't. It was only sex. We needed to get it out of our system. And we did."

"That was more than just sex, Kels, and you know it." I run a hand through my hair in frustration and she glances at me. "We have history together."

She stomps her foot and rolls her eyes. "There you go again, telling me what I know. Mansplaining things to me."

I swallow back the laugh and place a finger under her chin, gently guiding her to look at me.

"You're right. I'm sorry. The last thing I want is to continue to fight with you," I state, her eyes meeting mine. "Believe it or not, I still care about you."

She swallows and I fucking hate the pain I see behind her eyes. I put it there.

"There are things we should talk about, but...I just need some time to get my head straight," I try to explain. Her body visibly stiffens. "Can we at least try to be friends?"

She bites her bottom lip as she contemplates my offer. "You won't get all jealous and weird on me again, will you?"

Ugh, that's right. *Ben.*

I frown. "I can't make promises like that. But I'll try."

I hold out my hand. "Truce?"

She tilts her head to one side and then the other.

"Fine, whatever. Truce," she agrees, accepting my outstretched hand as we shake on it. Her hand remains connected with mine and when she doesn't pull away, I run my thumb over her knuckles. I watch goosebumps form on her arms before she finally jerks her hand from my grip.

I'm not sure what's going to happen next, but at least it's a start.

Chapter Thirteen

Kelsie

It's been a few days since the truce in the attic between Hayes and me.

It's had me thinking a lot about where things stand and how something has shifted between us. A weight that's been lifted. Not only the sexual tension that was so heavy—although for me, that hasn't dissipated in the least—but I've also felt the resentment I'd been holding disappear.

I'll begrudgingly admit that Lucy and Grace were right. If you learn to let go and to forgive someone, it can make a huge difference in how you feel.

In fact, I'm feeling so good after finishing the painting I've been working on, I asked Grace to come shopping with me. A new boutique opened up before the holidays that I've been dying to check out. Plus, I have a date scheduled this weekend with Ben, and I want to buy some sexy new underwear.

Okay, fine. It may not be Ben I want to impress with new panties. In fact, Ben and I haven't even gotten naked together yet. He's not seen any of my panty collection.

We've gone out twice now and although we've messed around, I always find an excuse not to go all the way with him. I don't know what's holding me back. I love sex and enjoy doing all the naughty things with a guy.

Ben is hot and a very good kisser. He has long fingers and a very nice tongue that have certainly done the trick of getting me off.

The hesitation seems to be that I don't have the chemistry with Ben that I do with Hayes.

Ben is not Hayes.

And it's messing with my head; not to mention my body.

That day Hayes and I fucked each other's brains out and then I left him for my date with Ben, my emotions were all over the friggin' place. I felt guilty because poor Ben was so sweet and thoughtful, and yet I wasn't really present with him and my head and heart weren't in it.

I left both back in my bedroom along with the memory of Hayes driving into me so fiercely I nearly blacked out from that amazing orgasm he gave me.

Maybe finding some new lingerie will get me in the mood for my upcoming date with Ben.

I pull into the driveway at the football house and Grace, already waiting for me on the front stoop, comes skipping down the front path. When she opens the door and slides into the passenger seat, she gives me one look and gasps in horror.

"Girl, what the hell is wrong with you? Are you okay?"

I furrow my brows. "What do you mean? Nothing's wrong."

She giggles and adjusts the rearview mirror down and motions for me to look at myself. I inhale sharply at the sight staring back at me.

"Holy shit! I'm a mess," I yelp, rubbing at all the paint smudges across my forehead and bridge of my nose. I left in a hurry after a quick painting session in the attic and didn't even bother to check myself in the mirror. I hurriedly changed into other clothes and ran out of the house to my car.

Grace pulls out a face wipe from her purse and hands it to me, and I swipe away the remnants of my artwork.

"Thanks," I say appreciatively, putting the car in reverse and backing out into the street. "I guess I've been a little distracted lately."

I'm not sure why I haven't said anything yet, but I haven't told Grace or Lucy about the hate-fucking I had with Hayes. Partially because they will both make a huge deal out of it and tell me that it means something is still there between us. All I want to do is move forward and forget about it.

That's hard to do when he is everywhere I am these days.

The other reason I haven't spilled the tea to my friends is because once I do, I know they'll dig and dig and dig until they uncover the real story.

Goddammit. I still love him.

And I hate myself for it.

"Do you want to talk about it?" Grace asks hesitantly, looking worried I might bite her head off. "Is it Hayes? Or Ben? Or something with your family?"

Yes. Yes. And all of the fucking above, yes.

I shake my head, but keep my eyes on the road as we head into town, leaving the quiet campus behind.

As if I'm a pot of water that's just reached its boiling point, I blurt out everything to my best friend. Well, almost everything.

"I fucked Hayes."

"You *what?*" she screeches, jolting upright in her seat and swiveling around to face me, grasping my thigh in her grip. "Oh, my God. Lucy totally called it! She just knew you would end up sleeping with him by the end of the semester."

I growl petulantly. "Argh! It's the last thing I wanted to do. I still hate him."

She clicks her tongue. "So you say...but your actions tell a completely different story."

I flip her off with my right hand and she giggles. I grip the steering wheel and curl my fingers around the leather so tight my knuckles turn white.

"Okay, fine. Maybe hate is a strong word, but I do hate myself for doing it. Especially when I'm seeing Ben."

"Ahh," she whispers introspectively. "Are you sleeping with both of them?"

I snort at the question. "No. And, technically, I'm not sleeping with Hayes either. It was a one-time thing and won't happen again. And Ben and I haven't had sex yet."

"Hmm...that's interesting."

I turn my head and give her a piercing look before returning my gaze to the road.

"What?" I snap sharply. "Spit it out, girly. Why is that so interesting?"

She's quiet for a moment, turning her attention out her window and without her having to say it, I already know what she's thinking.

If it weren't for Hayes and my messed-up romantic involvement with him, I probably would've already hooked up with Ben before now. I'm not shy about sleeping with guys. I like to have fun and enjoy the mutual and consensual satisfaction I get when I'm with someone I'm attracted to. I mean, case in point, I did sleep with Hayes the first night I met him in Paris.

"It seems to me that something—or *someone*—is holding you back from doing the deed with Ben."

I scoff like she's off her rocker even though I know she hit the nail on the head.

"Whatevs. Thanks for the talk, Dr. Ruth."

Grace pinches her lips together and her dark brows furrow. "Who's Dr. Ruth?"

I chuckle as I pull into a parking spot. The boutique is next to a flower shop, a bakery, and the best pizza shop in town called Bear-i-Cade Pizza. People in this town sure do like to use corny play on words with the CFU Bears team mascot.

As we open the door to the shop, we get a whiff of the delicious smelling pizza sauce from next door and my stomach grumbles.

"Let's pick up some pizza to bring back with us for dinner, okay?"

"Sounds good to me," Grace agrees. "You know I never say no to pizza."

She lets out a low whistle as she steps in behind me and sees the gorgeous clothes displayed on the racks in the store. "Wow. This stuff is beautiful."

I scan the shop, noticing what Grace does as I head straight back into the lingerie section.

"Welcome," a young woman greets. "Are you looking for something in particular?"

I smile and point to the drawers that are half-opened, displaying the mounds of undies and bra sets.

When all is said and done, I've purchased over $150 in new underwear and a brand new off-the-shoulder cream sweater that Grace said made me look angelic.

Which is ironic because I'm hoping to be anything but angelic when I wear it for Hayes.

I mean Ben.

Don't I?

Fuck.

I'm so confused.

Chapter Fourteen

Hayes

"Come on, man. Just come over," Hendy urges, his unshaven face peering at me through the video chat. I've been working for hours trying to finish a paper tonight and when his text messages were left unanswered, he decided to video call me. Apparently, not texting and responding to the great and powerful Joel Henderson equates to you being dead in a ditch somewhere. Who knew?

I groan and push back my desk chair in my room, the noise making a scraping sound as I stand. "Fine."

"Hells yeah! The game we're playing is fucking fire!" Killer yells from the background, then appears from around Hendy's back to wave, holding the controller in his hand, before turning his attention back to the entertainment happening on the TV screen.

Then I see Killer glance down, presumably reading a text, and announces with a grin. "Pizza's on the way."

Food. Yeah, I could be down with that.

"On my way too," I call out before hitting end on our video chat.

I leave my laptop and books scattered out on my desk and grab a jacket from my chair, walking at a fast-paced clip toward the football house.

When I enter their always chaotic residence, I find six of my teammates gathered in the living room making the noises you'd expect to hear from a bunch of dudes. Some you'd never want to hear in polite company.

Are they like this when the girls are around?

"Grab a chair from the kitchen," Hendy says, his eyes staying glued to the game that's clearly all combat and motions toward the kitchen.

"Guy coming at you from the northwest," Killer yells out to someone through a headset that looks to be way too small for his melon.

"Got 'em," EJ replies from a speaker sitting on the table.

"Watch your six."

"Where's EJ?" I ask, glancing around the room, confused why Emmett is on the phone and not down here playing with the rest.

Hendy uses a single finger to point up to the ceiling. "We only have two person on this one, so sometimes we split up and half of us play from here and half up in EJ's room," he explains.

"Oh. Makes sense." I've played some video games, but honestly most of my youth was spent out on a soccer field and not in front of a TV. It didn't leave a lot of time for anything else. Perhaps if I'd played more video games as a kid, I'd have the same interest as my friends and could bond more with everyone else.

I grab a chair and carry it back to the front room, taking

a seat to watch the action and the expressions on the players' faces. Killer is definitely the most animated. And loud.

As if hearing my thoughts, Killer leans down to a cooler next to his feet and, without missing a beat, tosses me a beer.

"Catch up."

"Thanks," I say with no argument and crack it open. It's been a long week and I need to let loose a little tonight.

"Pizza's here!" a female voice calls out from the front door. I glance behind my shoulder and see Grace stepping inside carrying two large pizza boxes.

Kelsie walks in behind her.

Shit.

Grace doesn't say anything as she enters, but she does smirk at me. Shit. I wonder what Kelsie told her. She sets down the pizza boxes on the coffee table.

"Get your fine ass over here, Soda Pop," Killer calls out to her in the sweetest tone I've ever heard the big dude use.

Grace smiles at her boyfriend and walks over to his open arms. Killer pulls her down into his lap with one hand and then circles it around her middle, all the while keeping his controller moving. Now that's talent. No wonder he's the leading tight end on the team last year.

"What'd you two do this afternoon?" he asks and then sniffs her. "You smell good. Is that new perfume?"

She giggles. "Yep. Kelsie and I went shopping at this new boutique on Main Street. I got perfume and she bought new lingerie."

My chest restricts and my stomach tightens into knots. Kelsie went lingerie shopping? My head snaps up and I steal a glance over at Kelsie, whose eyes quickly dart away when she catches my gaze on her.

Grace changes the subject. "You guys are still playing?"

"Fuck yeah. This game is awesome. Did you try it yet?"

"No. I had to finish a project last night," she explains. "Can I get next up? I'm gonna eat first."

"You bet, baby." Killer leans his chin on her shoulder and presses a kiss to her cheek. I don't normally get jealous when I see PDA from others, but right now a pang of envy stabs at my chest. I want that.

Does Kelsie feel it too? The longing and desire to go back to the way things were? God, I wish things had been different.

"Come sit down, Kels," Hendy says, patting the space between his legs. "I got a spot for you right here."

Red hot rage flashes in my veins. *Oh, hell no.*

I jump from my chair and motion toward mine with an outstretched hand.

"Here, you can have my seat, Kels. I'll get another one," I offer and hurry into the kitchen to grab another chair. When I come back in, Hendy raises a suspicious brow at me, but doesn't say anything.

I take a seat next to Kelsie and reach over her lap to grab a slice of pepperoni pizza from the box on the table. Without a second thought to what I'm doing, I hand her a piece before I grab another for myself.

"Thanks," she says appreciatively.

When I sit back down, my knee bumps against her thigh. Neither of us moves and I leave it to rest there.

Then we sit, side by side, eating our pizza and watching the game in a companionable silence, every once in a while joining in on the chorus of cheering for our friends when needed.

But, really, most of my attention is on the spot where her leg touches mine, where the heat of her penetrates through my jeans and pierces my skin.

What I wouldn't give to have her alone, to rip off her jeans and have my wicked way with her.

But that's only a dream.

* * *

I wake from my late afternoon nap with a start.

Sweat drips down my forehead in long, slick streaks. My heart races like I've just run out of oxygen after a marathon.

The nightmare I woke from isn't the one I normally have about the accident. This one is something new. It's about the night I left Paris.

I glance at my phone and realize I almost overslept. I have a telehealth video chat with my therapist in five minutes.

I roll out of bed and walk into the bathroom, using a washcloth to clean myself up before I throw on a pair of sweatpants and a CFU t-shirt. I shut my door and open the video app for my call.

"Hello, Hayes," Dr. Thompson says. "Is now still a good time for us to chat?"

"Hey, Dr. T," I reply and nod my head to proceed. "Yes, absolutely."

My parents made me start seeing Dr. Thompson after the accident. Both Holden and I were speaking with him separately and he prescribed both me and my brother anti-depression and anti-anxiety meds. Although I shouldn't have, I weaned myself off them when I was in Paris, but I wonder if I shouldn't be back on them.

"How are you doing this week?" he asks and it's a motherfucking loaded question.

I grimace. "I...may have had a slight panic attack recently."

"Oh, I see. Tell me what happened," he urges with an expression of concern, taking down some notes on his pad of paper.

I relay the story from the incident with Kelsie in the car. He's quiet as he listens closely, never interrupting me as I speak. When I finish the story, he leans forward in his chair and clasps his hands together in a prayer-like position in front of the screen.

"Well, it sounds like your friend really helped you out. Did you explain why you had the panic attack and what triggered you?" he asks in a non-judgmental tone.

I shrug. "I mean, I said I was in an accident..."

He gives me a pointed look. "Listen, Hayes. I know these things are very hard to talk about with me, much less anyone else. But it helps to be open about your feelings with the people you care about. Why do you think you haven't shared more with her?"

I groan and run a hand over my face. The stiff scrape of my jawline reminds me I need to shave. "Funny story, but she's the woman I was with and then left in Paris," I admit, knowing he is already well aware of Kelsie. He just doesn't know we're now at the same school.

He smiles sadly.

"I see. That makes things a bit uncomfortable?"

I give a short laugh. "You could say that."

Dr. T tilts his head to the side. "So things are not good between you two?"

"Not at first, no. She was pretty mad at me," I say and he nods at the camera. "But I think we've come to a truce in order to get along."

He adjusts his glasses on his nose. "Hmm...she has a right to her feelings and to be mad at you for doing what you did. In her perspective, she might think you did it on purpose because of something she did or didn't do. Perhaps, it's time you explain your sudden departure from Paris. That might help resolve things and reestablish your friendship."

I sigh. Dr. T makes it sound so easy. Just apologize. Just explain. Just get it all out in the open.

But in reality... it bites.

We spend the next forty-five minutes talking about my classes and how things are going with my brother. It's not life-altering conversation, but it's just nice to talk to someone, even if my parents are paying him to listen.

Once my time is up and we schedule for our next call, I decide to go downstairs and grab some dinner in the kitchen. I open my door and Kelsie nearly falls into my arms.

I reach out, grabbing her shoulders to steady her on her feet.

"Whoa there," I say as I make sure she's stable before releasing her. "What are you doing up here?"

She blushes and looks down at my feet. "I...was...shit, I was going to go up to the attic, walked by your door, heard what you said and I stopped and...I'm sorry. I shouldn't have eavesdropped. That was a private conversation," she says, the words tumbling from her mouth rapid fire as she looks everywhere but at my face.

"How long have you been listening?" I pluck her chin in my thumb and forefinger and drag her eyes to meet mine.

"A while," she confesses, her face turning a darker shade of pink.

Surprisingly, I'm not upset by this. Maybe it's the opening I've needed all along to finally bring everything to light with Kelsie. I drop my hand to hers and tug her behind me.

"Come on. I'm making us grilled cheese sandwiches and we are going to have this long-awaited talk."

She follows me down the stairs and I usher her into the kitchen where she takes a seat at the table and I pull out all the fixings to make us sandwiches. With my back turned to her, I feel a little less anxious. I can do this, I think to myself.

God, I hope I can do this. I hope I don't scare her away.

"A little over three years ago, my brother, Holden, our best friend, Kevin, and I were at a party. We hadn't had much to drink, and I wanted to leave. Since Kevin drank the least amount of beer, he said he'd drive. Not exactly the best way to assign a DD, but it is what it is. We all got in the car. I called shotgun and Holden got in the back behind Kevin. We were on the back roads not far from our home when Kevin lost control of the car and overcorrected. The car spun out and flipped into a ditch and flew right into a tree." I pause and glance over to gauge her expression.

She takes a sharp inhale of breath and her eyes grow wide in alarm. I turn back to the pan and flip the bread, taking a deep breath myself before continuing.

"Kevin died on impact..." I choke out the words. "He hadn't worn his seatbelt and was ejected through the front windshield. Holden got the brunt of the injuries because it was the driver's side that hit the tree."

I stop and take another breath, closing my eyes to shut out the images. It doesn't work. I can still see the scene of the accident. The front of the car busted and mangled, smoke pouring from the engine. Glass everywhere. Kevin lying face down in the ditch.

Kelsie remains quiet for a moment and then murmurs. "Oh, shit. Hayes, I'm so sorry."

I continue. "Even though it was three years ago, sometimes the memory is so fresh it feels like just yesterday. It changed our lives irrevocably. Holden deals with it sometimes worse than me. And the night I left you in Paris..." I drop my head and the threat of tears is real. I swipe the back of my hand over my eyelids, spatula still in my fist.

"I was so fucking worried about Holden. He was on the brink of a major meltdown. In a depressive spiral. He gets so dark sometimes and it consumes him. I'd spoken with him on the phone to wish him a Merry Christmas and...I knew. I knew if I didn't get home sooner than planned, he may have...Jesus, Kelsie. I didn't even think. I just...I needed to get home to him."

I turn off the stove burner and spin back around to face her, grasping the counter behind me for balance.

Kelsie is right there in front of me. She reaches up and cups my cheek. "I'm so sorry. I didn't know." She pauses before continuing. "Of course, your brother needed you."

"I'm so fucking sorry I left like that without an explanation. When I got home and spent time with him and he was fine, I...I didn't know what to say to you. I was ashamed of my behavior and honestly thought I'd never see you again so it didn't matter. I didn't call and I didn't reply. I guess I figured you'd said originally when we'd leave, we'd have a clean break," I say before taking a deep breath.

"And then...there you were. Now that I've seen you again, I realize what a horrible mistake I made. I know I can't change what I did, or didn't do... but, fuck, I want nothing more than to make it up to you," I add as I pull her against me. She doesn't fight it and I notice tears in her eyes as she looks up at me.

"I was really hurt when you left. That's why I acted like I did when we saw each other a few weeks ago. I wish I'd known what you were going through. I'm sorry I made that stupid three things rule in Paris. Shit, I'm sorry about a lot, Hayes," she whispers.

Fuck. I hate myself right now. Guess I know what to talk to Dr. Thompson about next time.

"I know, *mon amour*. I'm so sorry too," I apologize and frame her face in my hands, swiping a stray tear with my thumb.

"Please forgive me, Kelsie," I plead and press a gentle kiss to her forehead. I wrap my arms around her, pulling her more tightly against me.

When she lifts her arms to hug me back, I feel hope for the first time in a long time.

Chapter Fifteen

K elsie

The completeness I feel when I'm in Hayes's arms is something I've never felt before. He centers me. Grounds me. Makes me feel whole.

Which is why I slide my fingers through his and guide him out of the kitchen, down the hall, and into my bedroom.

"Kels?" he asks hesitantly, lifting his brows in question as I shut the door behind us and lean against it. I bite down on my lower lip, considering how I want to respond.

My emotions are all jumbled up in my head like cake batter in a mixer. What I've learned about Hayes in the last ten minutes has opened up a brand new perspective about who he is as a person and why he did what he did.

Am I still mad? A little.

It takes me a long-ass time to get over shit like this. Just ask my brother.

But what overrules that emotion is how much I want to comfort Hayes right now. To wipe away his pain and sorrow from that awful accident and the grief that followed and distract him the only way I know how.

I push off the door with the heel of my foot and stride three steps toward him, my eyes locked on his the entire time. I press the flat of my palm between his pecs hard enough that he stumbles backward and when his calves meet the bed frame, he falls back onto the bed.

"I accept your apology," I say, hovering over him as I place one knee on the mattress and the opposite hand on his shoulder, swinging my other leg over his lap. His eyes dart down his torso to where our bodies connect, his erection bulging between us as I give an experimental undulation of my hips. His gaze returns to mine and they flash a sexy note of appreciation, followed by a low groan when I do it again.

"Is this you forgiving me, then?"

I smile coyly, cocking my head to the side and licking my lips. "I don't know...it depends on how good the make-up sex is."

I laugh when he lifts his hips up hard enough to knock me off-balance. I steady myself with hands on his chest, my fingers moving lower to lift the hem of his T-shirt. When my fingers find the heat of his skin, I let out a sigh of relief.

"Sex between us has always been good, Kels," he states on a sexy punctuated moan.

I move my hands along the bare skin, roaming over the expanse of his chest, relishing in his heat. "That's never been a problem."

My fingers brush across the soft dusting of hair over his pectorals before I draw a path south, over the muscled ripples of his stomach down to the strip of hair that disappears under his waistband.

I choose not to respond with words and instead push the material of his shirt out of my way and lean down, flicking my tongue along the path my fingers took.

God, how I've missed this with him.

I plant wet kisses over the heat of his skin, skimming the sensitive flesh as I wedge my fingers under the waistband of his sweats and tug them down over his hips, past his knees, and down to his feet.

Before I can move to the floor to remove his briefs, Hayes catches my wrist in his hand and lifts his head to pin me with his stare.

"Not to ruin the moment, but I need to know...is Ben still in the picture?"

I shake my head and wiggle my way between his legs to land on my knees with my mouth inches from his protruding cock.

Ben and I met up last night and I broke it off with him, telling him I couldn't see him anymore. He seemed okay with it, but did ask me if it was because of Hayes. I couldn't lie and confirmed his suspicions were correct.

Our eyes lock and for a second, I want to spill every-thing. How I was never into Ben and it was always him who had my heart.

Still has my heart.

"I ended things with Ben last night."

Hayes props himself up on his elbows, a slow smile itching at the corners of his mouth.

"Good," he says with satisfaction. "So, what are you waiting for?"

I give him a dirty smirk and free his erection from his briefs.

The sight of his beautiful cock has my mouth watering. His straining erection bobs before me and my pussy clenches with the need to be filled; missing the connection. But first I want to taste him.

I wrap his length in my fist and bend forward, swiping

the crown of his dick with the tip of my tongue, breathing in his musky, spicy essence. My panties grow damp as I remember our first time together in Paris. How when I took him in my mouth, he praised me endlessly as I brought him to orgasm.

My eyes flutter as I lick the length of his cock with the flat of my tongue and I can't help but murmur in French.

"*Tu me manques, mon amoureux.*" Which roughly translates to mean *I've missed you, lover.*

Hayes flashes a devious smile, reaching behind my head to clasp my hair in his hand.

"*Moi, aussi,*" he says, and then tugs my head back so my mouth falls open on a gasp. "Now take me in your mouth, *mon amour.*"

I'm not sure if it's his use of the French language, the desire in his handsome grin, or the dirty command that sends sparks of arousal between my legs, but it is the sexiest request I've ever heard. I comply immediately.

In an instant, his length fills my open mouth, my lips stretched wide to accommodate his girth. I slide him over my tongue until he hits the back of my throat. I gag and swallow, my eyes watering from the delicious intrusion.

"Oh fuck, baby," he mutters in a raspy tone and I smile around him. "I've missed you so much."

His words encourage me as I suck him in and out, swirling my tongue over the head and using my hand to stroke him hard. I glance up at his face and see his half-lidded eyes are glazed over with lust and his grip tightens on my hair, yanking the strands to produce a lusty moan from my throat.

The vibration of the moan seems to increase his pleasure and I do it again, feeling his thighs tighten around me.

His cock twitches and then the taste of salty cum floods my mouth.

"*Coming*," he sputters, arching off the bed, hips pistoning faster as he releases ropey strands of hot orgasm to the back of my throat. I swallow and breathe through my nose as he finishes with a gravelly growl before he collapses back on the bed.

I pull off, wiping my mouth with my fingers as I rise up and slide next to him on my mattress. Hayes turns his head to face me, his expression serene and content.

If I could paint him right now, I would. His expressive face is so beautiful and says everything I want to hear without words.

He lifts a thumb to my cheek, sliding it over my cheekbone to tuck a fallen lock behind my ear.

"*Tu es tres belle*," he says softly and I lean into his palm.

I give him a provocative smile. "You're only saying that because I just made you come with my mouth."

Hayes drops his hand, depressing his thumb into my bottom lip before he pushes it inside. I lick the pad with the tip of my tongue that moments before had been coated with him.

He shakes his head, removes his thumb, and leans down to cover my mouth with his. The kiss is sweet and tender, but quickly turns hot and combustible.

Hayes slides his tongue between my lips at the same time he rolls on top of me, his semi-erect cock wedging between my legs.

When he pulls away, he stares into my eyes as if searching for something. I flutter my lashes and lick my lips, the taste of him still lingering.

"You are the most beautiful woman I've ever known," he says, the sincerity in his tone piercing my heart wide open. "And I'm going to worship every inch of your body until you believe me."

I stretch my arms out wide and let him undress me until I'm completely naked and he stares down at me with an appreciative gaze.

"Let's see what you got, lover."

Chapter Sixteen

Hayes

I let my eyes roam over Kelsie's body, taking in the exquisite canvas of her creamy soft skin. It's like unwrapping a Christmas gift that you've wanted the entire year. No matter how many times I see her like this, it's never enough.

It'll never be enough.

"Hayes?" Kelsie murmurs as she gives me an expectant look, her teeth biting at the corner of her mouth.

I press a finger to her lips. "Patience, *mon amour*. I'm deciding where I want to start," I whisper.

"Am I that big of a puzzle?"

"You're not a puzzle. You're more like a dessert buffet," I state with a quirk of a smile. Then I bend down and press a chaste kiss to her lips. Slowly, I kiss and lick down her jawline and long, slender neck before I make up my mind.

Slipping off the bed, I stand up and tug her feet toward me. She gives me a curious look, but doesn't say anything as I take her right ankle in my hand and bring it up to my shoulder. I press a kiss to the inside of her ankle and run my tongue along her calf muscle. I repeat this on her other ankle and leg. She doesn't protest or move.

I love that about Kelsie. She's not bashful about her sexuality or body and I love her confidence in the bedroom. I love how we both take charge, like playing a game against a worthy opponent where the ball goes back and forth between each of us.

I push her feet to the edge of the bed with her knees up, pull her hips toward me, and I drop to my knees on the floor, just as she did for me. I bite the inside of her thigh and she moans. My girl enjoys it a little rough, which is good because when I'm with her, I often lose control.

I flick my tongue over the same spot along the crease between her folds and thigh. I repeat this and her hands bunch the sheets next to her hips. It makes me smile against her skin as I kiss her neatly-trimmed patch of dark blonde hair just above her core.

Her hands fly off the covers and land on my head, gripping at my hair. "Hayes!" she growls.

"What did I say about patience, *mon amour?*" I chastise with the snick of my teeth.

She groans and flops back as I continue with my ministrations. Using my thumbs, I slowly separate her folds, revealing that glistening pink skin that I've become so intimately familiar with this past year. Every square inch of her is utter perfection, as if her body was sculpted straight from my fantasies.

I let the flat of my tongue glide over her entrance, circling it with the tip. She thrusts her hips upwards, desperately seeking more. When I finally flick over her swollen clit, she trembles underneath me with a cry. I lick down her folds and spear her entrance with my tongue.

"Yes," she whimpers, fisting her hands tightly in my hair.

I replace my tongue with two fingers, sinking them inside her wet heat, feeling her muscles contract around them. It takes all my willpower not to slam my cock inside instead. Fuck, she feels good like this, compliant and quivering.

I double my efforts by licking and sucking her clit until her inner muscles start to spasm.

She groans when I pull my fingers free.

"I'm so close, baby," she protests, squirming on the bed for more. "Don't be a tease."

"Patience," I remind her yet again with a smile as I lean forward once more and flick her clit with my tongue. She moans as I slide my tongue lower and work it in and out of her until she's crying out my name.

"I want that pretty pussy clenching down on my cock when you come again," I growl against her clit as I kiss it once more.

I hear her suck in a breath. If there's one thing Kelsie loves in the bedroom, it's dirty talk.

"Condom?"

She points me in the direction of her nightstand drawer where I find a full pack. When I give her a quizzical look, she lifts a shoulder coyly.

"They give them out on campus like lollipops at a doctor's office. You can never be too prepared," she explains as I tear off a foil packet from the strip.

I rip it open with my teeth and slide it over my straining cock. She shimmies back up the mattress to make room for me as I settle between her thighs. With my cock in hand, I line up with her entrance and slowly enter her hot, wet flesh. We both release a collective sigh as inch by perfect inch, I'm fully seated inside her body.

I remain still for a moment relishing in the tight heat of her. Kelsie grunts out in exasperation and clenches around me, grabbing my ass in her palms.

"I've waited long enough. Hurry up and make me come before I die from lack of orgasms," she demands with a punctuating eye roll.

Fuck, I love her smartass mouth.

I lean down and kiss her as I slowly roll my hips and begin to move, sliding my hands under her thighs. I push them forward to press them against her body, giving me leverage to sink deeper. She closes her eyes and moans.

Grabbing a pillow, I place it under her ass as we continue to kiss, knowing exactly what angle she needs. I begin to move faster and harder, and she closes her eyes as her mouth drops open in pleasure.

I take her hands in one of mine and hold them against the mattress above her head as I tilt my pelvis with a deep thrust while pressing a thumb to her clit, and that's what propels her over the edge. Her entire body trembles beneath me, her inner muscles undulating around my dick.

"Fuck, Kels!" I scream as she calls out my name, both of us finding our release together.

I pull out after a moment and discard the used condom before pulling her against my side. She drops a kiss to the center of my chest and then lays her head down, snuggling into me.

"God, that felt good," she sighs out.

I kiss the top of her head in reply. "We're pretty good together."

"Yes, we are," she agrees and I tighten my hold on her. "I think we may have surpassed the truce."

"Yeah, I think we've had a ceasefire and we're in peace-time now, baby."

* * *

I'm not sure what time I fell asleep last night, but it was after several rounds of fucking. Thank God I don't have practice or training this morning.

When not making each other orgasm, Kelsie and I talked straight through into the early morning hours, sharing things about ourselves we've never told one another before. There's a lot we don't know about each other yet because of the "only three things" rule we stupidly enacted in Paris.

Based on what little she told me last night, it sounds like she might have a strained relationship with her family, but she didn't go into much detail and I didn't push her. She talked a lot about the time she spent with her aunt in Paris.

We fell asleep lying side by side, staring into each other's eyes.

When I slowly wake, my eyes blinking to adjust to the bright light from the window, I notice Kelsie's gone. What the hell?

I find my clothes, throw on my pants, and open the door to her bedroom, peering down the hallway but don't see or hear anything.

"Kelsie?" I call out quietly, padding into the kitchen and front room before I make my way upstairs.

When I get to the attic stairs, I hear something. I walk up and turn the corner, grinning when I find her swaying her ass back and forth as she paints on a canvas. She has earbuds in and is clearly listening to music, humming along to it as she paints. I lean against the wall to watch her.

This is the true Kelsie. She is more herself here than anywhere else...well, besides the bedroom.

I step closer to look at her painting and she jumps, pulling out an earbud.

"Jesus Christ, Hayes! You have to stop sneaking up on me like that," she yelps, throwing a hand in the air.

I laugh and try to get a good look at what she's working on, but she steps in front of it. "It's not done yet," she protests.

I hold up my hand to cover my eyes. "Okay. I won't look."

She laughs and nudges me in the shoulder. I drop my hand and take in her appearance.

She's wearing her pair of painting overalls with nothing underneath. The curve of her breast is visible against the well-worn bib. Fuck, that's hot.

Clearing my throat—and my thoughts—I turn toward the wall and see a painting that grabs my attention. It's a CFU logo football helmet on the field.

Kelsie follows the direction of my gaze. "Grace asked me to paint one for Killer's birthday gift."

"I like it. Can I commission some art?" I ask.

She glances over at me and purses her lips. "I suppose. What'd you have in mind?"

I saunter over to her and she places her brush and palette down as I wrap my arms around her waist and kiss her gently.

"You...naked?" I tease with a smirk.

She smacks my chest playfully and I smile. I love when she's like this with me, carefree and fun. I wish I could make her feel this way all the time.

"How about our trip to Nice?" I ask, being more serious.

"I can do that," she whispers against my jaw.

"You're really good at this." I pause as I remember something. "Hold on. I saw something on campus a few days ago and I meant to tell you about it." I pull my phone from my sweatpants pocket and find the link, pulling it up on the screen.

I hold it out for her to read.

"When I saw it, I immediately thought of you. You've probably already heard about the annual art competition for the university."

"I don't know, Hayes. That's like for real art students. I..." She trails off, her eyes drifting over the nearly dozen canvases in the room.

I tilt her chin up with my finger and thumb to look at me. "You are a real artist, *mon amour*. You are so talented. At least consider it."

She bites her lip and I pull it free with my thumb. "You. Are. Talented," I state again as I search her eyes, wondering where my strong woman has gone. I feel like there's more behind this sudden lack of self-confidence that is so out of character for her.

"Breakfast?" she asks as if sensing that I'm going to ask more questions. I cock my head to the side, considering whether to push this conversation or let it go for now.

I pick her up and she wraps her legs around my waist. "I'm hungry...but not for breakfast," I say as I nip her collarbone.

"Consider me your personal buffet," she whispers as I carry her downstairs to my bedroom.

"Is it an all-I-can-eat buffet?"

I will never get my fill of her.

Chapter Seventeen

K elsie
"Hey, you have a weird look on your face. What's going on?"

I lift my head from the milkshake I've been nursing and find Grace scrutinizing me with a suspicious look in her eyes.

"You're the weird one," I counter in a sassy tone, sticking my tongue out at her. "Nerdy STEM girl."

Grace throws her head back with a laugh, knowing I'm only joking and how proud I am of her achievements. She recently won an award from some prestigious development company for a software design she submitted for their annual conference. There is no doubt in my mind that she will go far after college graduation considering all the job offers she already has on the table.

It has me thinking a lot about the art contest Hayes mentioned the other day and whether I should enter a piece.

I decide to seek Grace's advice on the subject.

"Hayes wants me to enter the art contest, but I don't know if I want to."

Grace's spoon clatters to her plate. "What? Of course you should! Sugar Smacks, your work is incredible. Why would I have asked you to paint Killian's birthday present if I didn't think so?"

I scoff. "Killer has no taste. I mean, come on. The guy drinks warm beer and thinks that's delicious."

Grace chuckles. "*Touché*. Bad example. But I think your work is amazing and you shouldn't hide it away from the world."

"I don't," I argue, but she glowers with a look that says *you're such a liar*. "You know my art is just for me. It helps me process things. Deal with my feelings. I'm not hiding it intentionally."

Well, maybe I am.

It's a bone of contention and the reason I'm not speaking to my brother any longer.

As if she reads my mind, Grace cocks her head and purses her lips together, shrewdly assessing me. I swear the girl can see directly into my soul.

"Does this have to do with your brother and dad?"

Maybe. *Yes.* "No," I say with an adamant snort. "It has nothing to do with them."

She reaches an arm across the table and grabs my hand in hers. I try to pull it away, but she doesn't let go. Considering how much smaller she is than me, that girl is stronger than I give her credit for. I let out a resigned sigh.

"I think it does, Kels. I think you're scared to really pursue your dreams of being an artist because your dad has messed with your head and has you by the short hairs."

I shake my head and pull my hand out from hers, placing it down on my lap. Grace knows all about what happened to me two years ago when I cut out my brother from my life.

It was a betrayal of trust when he went behind my back and told my parents about my plans and ruined everything. That disloyal motherfucker.

When we were kids, my older brother, Keaton, was my hero. We did everything together because he was the only one ever there for me and had my back.

Our parents were always gone, traveling the world. My dad owns an international fashion company and my mom didn't want to stay home and take care of the kids. So we were left alone to be raised by a slew of nannies.

Grace is partially right. I'm in school pursuing a degree in International Business because my dad holds the purse strings and said he'd cut me off if I went in the direction of art school and not a business degree.

"I just need to finish my program and then I can do what I want," I state with a stiff nod, stuffing a fry in my mouth and smiling tightly.

Grace lets out a sigh of resignation, knowing it's useless to try and argue with me when my mind is made up. I'm stubborn as fuck and I'm doing what I have to until I reach twenty-five. That's when I inherit the money my grandparents left me and I'm a free woman. Until then, I'll keep my head down, focus on my studies, and enjoy making art for myself and my own personal collection which continues to grow with every piece I finish.

"Hear me out on this, Kels," Grace says, wiping a napkin over her mouth before she smiles deviously and leans forward, giving me a pointed look. "Wouldn't that be the ultimate act of revenge?"

I pull my head back and narrow my brows. "Revenge? For who?"

She points a finger at me. "You. Unless I'm mistaken, your dad's only stipulation was that he'd pay for your education *only* if you studied international business, right?"

"Yeah."

"But he never said you couldn't do art at all. So *do it*. Submit something great to this contest. Don't let him take the joy and fun out of life. Think of it as the biggest FU to your dad."

I throw my head back and cackle loudly. "When the hell did you become such a badass bitch?"

Grace flips a lock of her long dark hair and gives me a cheeky grin. "I learned from the best."

Hayes and I have been working on our project for the past hour, diligently scrubbing through our interview notes and drafting our final outline. Now we're at a point where the rubber meets the road and we have to begin writing our paper...but I'm bored out of my mind and don't want to do any of that right now. There's only one thing I want to do at the moment, and that's *Hayes*.

I stare at him with his back propped up against my headboard, knees up with his laptop balanced on his thighs as he types something in our shared Google doc.

He's so sexy when he concentrates on his work. It's what drew me to him initially the first time I saw him in the busy café in Montmartre, across the street from Moulin Rouge. I remember that day so vividly.

The guy I've been watching for the last fifteen minutes wears an adorable look of confusion across his face, his brows furrowed as he stares over a Parisian street map as if it's completely foreign to him. Because of the way his head is bent, his dark, wavy hair falls over his eyes, framing his face. Every few seconds he pushes it behind his ear. Without even speaking to him, I know he must be American and is probably on a summer trip, or maybe a gap year, and definitely a little lost.

As if he feels me staring at him, he lifts his gaze to meet mine. I smile and give a small fluttery wave of my fingertips. Then I stand up, grab my bag and coffee, and stroll over to his table with one intent—to find out if he is free later.

"You look like you need some help," I offer confidently, speaking in English. I pull out the wicker café chair and sit down without waiting for an invitation.

He appraises me dubiously, his eyes assessing me with great curiosity. "If you're offering, then yes, I need some help."

And that was that. Hayes and I finished our coffees over a brief introduction and then I began giving him the tour of the quartier of Montmartre. It ended with us naked in bed in my flat later that evening.

I thought it would be a one-night thing and I'd never see him again. But fate had other plans and Hayes ended up in my International Business course at the university in Paris. It was the most beautiful time of my life.

I sigh at the memory and push my laptop to the side of the bed, stretching my arms over my head. I get to my knees and crawl over to his side, his dark eyes lifting from his laptop and landing on me.

"What's up?" he asks, cocking his head to the side, eyebrows raised. When he gets a good look at my hungry expression, he nods. "Oh...in need of a study break?"

I simply nod and pull my T-shirt up over my head and toss it to the floor, leaving me in my pink, see-through bra and booty shorts.

Reaching for his laptop, I shift it off his lap and set it next to mine. He drops his knees and stretches his legs out to allow me to straddle him. As I do, Hayes reaches around my backside to cup my ass in his hands, jerking me forward. Nestled in the juncture of my legs, I feel the very evident bulge of his cock under the material of his track pants.

Without a word, I burrow my hands underneath his T-shirt and lift it up to expose the divine structure of his abdominals and chest. He dutifully raises his arms as I divest him of his shirt.

His body is perfectly sculpted, his long torso covered with a soft dusting of dark hair. He's not big like other football players because of his position on the team. His physique is more lean and not bulky, but his muscles are toned and defined. I run my fingers through the trail of hair and then up over his chest, scoring a fingernail over the round, copper penny nipple. I feel his cock jerk in response between my legs.

A swath of his wavy hair falls casually over his forehead and I brush it away before leaning down to kiss him.

It's slow and exploratory. He moves his hands to cup my jaw and our mouths open for each other and I sweep my tongue inside before sealing my lips over his.

Hayes's long, tapered fingers return to clutch the globes of my ass, digging into my flesh as they move my hips in a rocking motion.

I withdraw from the kiss and sit upright, unhooking my bra and letting it fall away, my breasts now hanging bare between us. Hayes leans forward and flicks one of my nipples with the tip of his tongue and I arch forward. The sensation creates a ripple of need that shoots straight to my clit.

I rock my hips lazily back and forth, the rhythm picking

up speed when he cups my breasts in his palms, sucking them one at a time.

"Mmm..." I moan, unable to contain the pleasure that each stroke of his tongue produces. "I need you inside me. Now."

We wrangle out of our remaining clothes and I readjust myself on top of him, the silky length of him gliding over my wet slit.

Taking him in hand, I circle the engorged head with my fingers, smoothing the pearls of wetness around his crown. He growls and I peer down at where the head of his cock nestles between my folds.

Rising up on my knees, I angle my hips so his tip is at my entrance. I return my gaze to his, finding his eyes dark with lust, unfocused, and heavy-lidded. Before he can say a word, I slam down, impaling myself on his cock.

"Wait..." Hayes tries to scramble up on his hands, but I shake my head, pushing him back down with my palms over his pecs.

"Shhh...let me just ride you like this. We're okay."

The look in his eyes moves from concern over our protection to blissed-out satisfaction as I roll my hips forward, taking him further inside.

"Oh fuck, Kels...you're going to ruin me."

My only response to his admission as we take each other to the promised land is, "*Good.*"

Chapter Eighteen

Hayes

We lie naked and spent in each other's arms, neither of us speaking for what feels like forever.

Kelsie trails her finger over a scar I have on my thigh from the accident.

"The windshield shattered," I state as I watch her index finger pause over the raised flesh that puckers in an ugly zigzag even after several years.

She looks up at me. "Did it hurt?"

I shake my head. "I don't really remember. Everything happened so fast and I was in shock."

She leans her head back against my chest. "I'm sorry that happened to you. And I'm sorry about the loss of your friend."

I tense a little and instead of pulling away, she presses a kiss to my collarbone. I wrap my arms more tightly around her. I'm not ready to share my guilt yet, but she deserves to know more.

"Holden, my brother, has never completely recovered—

physically or mentally," I admit, forcing myself to take a deep breath.

"He's lucky to have you," she says quietly and goes back to drawing circles around my scar.

"I don't know about that...but I thank God every day we both lived. I don't know what I would have done if I'd lost both Holden and Kevin."

The confession has me fighting back tears that threaten to spill.

Kelsie sighs as she runs her finger up my side and tilts her head slightly up toward mine. "I wish I was still close to my brother."

My body stills beneath her. This is the first time she's said anything remotely emotional about her family and I haven't wanted to pry. Hell, maybe that's our biggest issue... neither one of us wanted to get too close.

"What happened between you two?" I ask, rubbing her back lightly as she traces each of my abdominal muscles.

"He broke my trust," she says and I glance down to see her press her lips tightly together. I give her a squeeze and she wraps her arm around me and squeezes back.

"How?"

She sucks in a deep breath and then exhales before she continues.

"It's a long story...but my dad owns a women's fashion company, which meant my parents traveled all over the world for months at a time and left us alone a lot as kids. It was just Keaton and me, and usually a nanny. But we always had my Aunt Desiree, my dad's sister. She's the black sheep of the family and I adored her." Kelsie lifts her chin and smiles.

Having met her aunt, I know how much love they have for each other and I nod.

"Before she moved to France, she lived near us in San Francisco until she hit it big with her art and then she moved. I was devastated, but Keaton and I got to spend time with her each summer when she taught us about the art world. I fell in love with it and knew it was what I was meant to do with my life."

She grows quiet for a moment and I don't press further, but want to know why she isn't pursuing it now if it makes her so happy.

"At the time, my parents didn't care about my interests —until I was a sophomore in high school. That summer, Desiree wanted to send me to an art camp. But Keat fucked it all up for me and went behind my back to tattle on me to our dad. That was the beginning of the end for my relationship with Keaton and the reason I'm here at CFU and not in art school."

"What happened? Why couldn't you do what you wanted to do?" I question, pressing a kiss at her temple.

"Keaton ratted me out and my dad forbade me to go to the camp. He said he'd only pay for me to attend business school and not waste money on art. His dream is for us to take over the company someday."

"And that was that?" I ask, surprised that the Kelsie I know would follow that ultimatum. The Kelsie I know has a stubborn streak and can be willful about rules and boundaries when she wants something. "So you just complied with his demands?"

She laughs ruefully. "No, not exactly. My aunt ended up paying for the art course and signed the release, since I was still seventeen. I was all set to begin. Keaton knew about it, and instead of supporting me, he intentionally went behind my back *again* and told my parents. Of course, they were furious that she would do that without their permission. So I got shipped home early and had to start school here that fall."

She finishes the story and her head lies limply against my chest in what seems like defeat.

"I'm so sorry, *mon amour*," I murmur against the crown of her head. "But you're here and you found a way to get to France on your own. I'm proud of you."

I feel wetness from a tear that drops from her eyes.

"Maybe, but it still hurts. My brother betrayed me. He knew how much art and going to that camp meant to me. He was so fucking blinded by family duty bullshit that he didn't even consider my dreams. He took away an opportunity to do what I loved. In the process, he killed our relationship by stabbing me in the back and leaving me with nothing." Her voice cracks on the last word, and that breaks my fucking heart.

"Oh, baby, I'm so sorry. I wish you would have told me all this before," I offer sympathetically, as I roll her underneath me. I wipe a stray tear from her cheek and try to kiss away the pain she's clearly still in.

Just like me.

This explains so much about why she didn't want to get too close. I thought it was just her carefree attitude and she simply wanted to have fun while in Paris, but now it all makes sense.

Her trust was broken by the one person she believed in more than anyone. I swallow hard, understanding better now why it gutted her so deeply when I left her in Paris without an explanation. And it explains why she's been so fucking guarded since I arrived at CFU. I have half a mind to pummel Keaton if I ever meet him for what he's done to her.

"I wish we would have told each other everything when

we were in Paris. I'm sorry I made that stupid three things only rule," she says, our mouths inches from each other.

I push up on my palms and smile down at her, arching a brow.

I press a kiss to her mouth before bending my head down to kiss her breast and then moving down her abdomen. "I have a new three things rule," I say as I place a wet kiss to her clit. "Three things I want to kiss on Kelsie's body."

She giggles, but her laughter fades as I slide two fingers inside her.

"I think I like your new three things rule."

I grin against her wet flesh. "Then you'll really like this."

* * *

"Why do we have to do three things?" she asks as we walk down the quad with ice cream cones in our hands.

"Because three things games are our thing," I point out as I lick a drop of ice cream from my waffle cone.

"But we could just tell each other everything we like and don't like," she states as she licks her strawberry ice cream.

"Nah...that's no fun. Also, I can't believe we are eating ice cream in the winter while walking outside," I say with a laugh.

"Hey, you wanted a date where we did three things we each like, and you got to pick dinner, which I'm still questioning," she retorts.

I smirk. When I suggested we have a date day where we each pick three things we like that have to be incorporated into the date, I may have been excited to pick our meal of chili cheese dogs from the local diner. They are my absolute favorite food.

"You picked seeing that super-predictable romance movie," I groan as we continue walking toward the football house.

"Well, you chose those chocolate mint candies instead of popcorn at the theater, which is total movie blasphemy."

"Junior Mints are the only kind of candy you should ever get at the theater!" I scoff, pretending to be offended.

"Right," she replies, drawling out the word.

"At least it's warm out today, I mean for winter in the mountains," I add as we cross the street, and I step around Kelsie to be between her and traffic.

"So what's your third thing?" she asks.

"The guys are having a get-together and they invited us to play some flag football in the back yard," I say as we walk up to the house. I stuff the remaining bite of waffle cone in my mouth and chew.

"Oh, hell no...I'm not playing football!" she protests as she eats the last of her cone.

"Yes, you are," I declare. I cock my head to one side. "What's your third thing?"

She winks at me. "My third thing doesn't involve clothes." She giggles and tries to make a run for it up the stairs, but I grab her and toss her over my shoulder, slapping her ass as I walk up the front steps.

"Put me down!" she squeals with a laugh.

"Not a chance, baby. Not a chance."

I never want to put this woman down. I'm not sure what's happening between us, but I sure as hell hope it doesn't stop. I haven't thought of anything bad in days and it's all thanks to how Kelsie makes me feel.

Alive.

Chapter Nineteen

Kelsie

"So...you and Mac, huh?" Hendy asks me as we leave our team huddle and position ourselves at the line of scrimmage to wait for the snap. He'd seen us show up at the house earlier when Hayes carried me in over his shoulder, his hand on my ass.

I'd not always been a fan of public displays of affection from other couples, especially when they get to the point where they should get a room, but I kind of liked the way Hayes kept his hands on me and made it very obvious we were together. We hadn't officially said anything to anyone about our relationship, but I certainly got the eyeballs from Grace and Lucy when they saw us.

I lift a shoulder noncommittally and play coy in response to his question. "Maybe."

He bumps his shoulder against mine, a frown marring his normally perfect face. "I thought you said you'd never date a football player."

I bend over at the waist and take my spot facing my opponent, Lucy, who is trying her best to look tough and ready to fight. Hendy readies himself next to me and I chuckle.

"That was just my way of telling you I didn't want to date *you*."

Hendy scoffs and glances at me, my statement catching him off-guard so when the ball is snapped from Killer, he fumbles the ball in his hands. It leaves just enough room for our opponents to get the upper hand.

EJ rushes over the makeshift line in the back yard of the house and moves in straight toward Hendy. Killer tries to block him, but is pushed off-balance when Grace tries to tackle him in a hug, which is comical because she's maybe five foot two and barely 110 pounds and Killian is a giant. But her distraction does the trick and Emmett finds his target, leaping around me and grabbing for Hendy's flag hanging from his track pants.

"Yaaas!" EJ shouts as he grabs the ball from Hendy's hands and lifts it up in the air, doing a goofy, uncoordinated dance of victory. Lucy runs up to him and throws her arms around his waist.

"Killer!" Hendy grouses, shoving his buddy in the shoulder with his palm. "Do you call that protection? I can't imagine what you would've done if Gracie had flashed you her boobs."

Killer grins and then looks down at Grace smiling up at him. He waggles his eyebrows at the suggestion. "Not a bad idea, Soda Pop. Next time..."

Grace slaps him on the chest with a huff. "My boobs are only for you in private."

"Timeout!" Killian announces, grabbing Grace's wrist to pull her toward the house. "My girl just said she'd show me her boobs...gotta go!"

A chorus of chuckles and 'boos' go up as we watch

Killer and Grace stride toward the back door of the house. When I turn my head, I see Hayes watching me, a dark look in his eyes. I know what that expression means. I cock an eyebrow and shake my head, mouthing the word, "*Later.*"

Our teams disperse at the call for timeout as Killer and Grace leave and I head to the deck chairs on the back patio where there's a fire blazing in the pit. This winter has been a mild one with very little snow, but there is a chill in the late afternoon air.

I shiver and cross my arms, watching the flames as they fan out in the breeze, sparking and sizzling, when I feel an arm around my shoulder.

"You cold?" Hayes asks and I lean into the warmth of his body, turning my face to bury my nose in his sweatshirt. I inhale a deep breath, my body stirring from his musky and spicy scent.

I unfold my arms and wrap them around his waist. He feels so good. This *feels* so good between us.

Now that we've started to share a little bit more about each other's lives and what led us here, I realize that a weight has been lifted from my heart. I guess Lucy and Grace know what they're talking about when it comes to letting things go and learning to forgive. Maybe one or both of them should change majors and go into psychology because they nailed it.

I'm about to suggest to Hayes that we take off and follow in Killian and Grace's footsteps when Emmett, Lucy, and Hendy join us around the fire.

Lucy gives me a look that clearly shows both her interest in this new development and her displeasure that I've kept this secret from her and hadn't mentioned anything before now.

She wiggles her pointer finger at Hayes and my joined

bodies. "Okay, spill the tea. What's going on here? I thought you had a very strong dislike for him."

I pull back from Hayes's embrace, lifting my gaze to him before turning it back on Lucy.

"Maybe I did…but he's grown on me. The short version is we've been fucking," I say, waiting for Hayes to argue this point. Right on cue, he snorts and adds his commentary.

"We're *dating*." He squeezes my arm and tucks me in close again. I laugh at his expected response, but gaze up at him appreciatively. Hayes tips his head down and we lock eyes. His tell me he wants more, but I'm not sure if I'm ready for that just yet. Then Hayes turns back to Lucy. "It's new. We're picking up where we left off in Paris."

Hendy coughs. "What happened to the hockey player, Kels?"

I know Hendy's not being a dick by asking the question, but Hayes doesn't know that. I feel him stiffen in my arms and I try to ease his jealousy by rubbing a hand down his back.

"Catch up, Henderson. That's yesterday's news. I'm not the one with a revolving door like some people I know."

Hendy drops the subject with a grunt, knowing I'm referring to him and his conquests. We love to tease him about his *girl du jour*. Someday he'll find the girl who will make him fall head over heels for her. Maybe.

Lucy rolls her hoodie sleeve up to look at her watch. "It's been fifteen minutes. I think we should call it a game because I don't think there's a snowball's chance in hell Killer and Grace are making another appearance tonight."

"That's my boy," Emmett chuckles and then reaches for Lucy's hand, sliding his fingers through hers. "We should get going too. I have to check on my grandma and make sure she's okay."

Lucy nods and then leans in toward me, giving me a side hug goodbye. "You better call me later."

I hug her back. "I will. Promise."

Hendy glances at Hayes and me, grimaces at what he sees. "Nah...you guys can't ditch me too."

Hayes shrugs. "Sorry, bro. But it was fun. Thanks for asking us to play."

"Cheer up, Hendy," I say, patting him on the shoulder. "I'm sure your contacts are filled with girls who will gladly come keep your lonely ass company. And I bet they won't mind if you tackle them either."

Hayes laughs and Hendy grumbles, fishing out his phone from his pocket and flipping through his contacts list. "Yeah, I guess. But I like hanging out with you guys. Are you sure you can't stay for another beer? I'll buy the pizza."

Hayes shakes his head and thumps his team captain on the back. "Next time, man. I'll see you tomorrow for our scrimmage."

As we head out the side yard through the gate, hand in hand toward our own house, I nestle into Hayes's arm, one hand clasped over his bicep.

"You passed up free pizza for me. Wow. I feel pretty special." My tone is teasing, but Hayes stops us in the middle of the sidewalk, holding my chin in his fingers.

"You are special, Kelsie. And for the record, we *are* dating."

He leans down and kisses my forehead, leaving me with a smile on my face the entire walk home.

Chapter Twenty

Hayes

The twilight sky dances with the last purple and orange strands of sunlight as Kelsie and I walk to the top of the hill where our house faces a mountain vista. Kelsie draws to a halt at the end of our walkway, pulling me to a stop with her. I look down at our joined hands and smile as I absently run my thumb alongside hers.

It's taken all of my willpower not to throw her over my shoulder and hurry us back home. These last few days have felt magical, like some sort of healing balm has covered my emotional wounds. I feel more alive, living in the present and not in the past.

I've been more focused with my football training and my coursework. Kelsie does something to me, and now that I've begun to open up to her, it's as if we've reached a whole new level in our relationship. We've summited a mountain and the view is so much better than I ever thought it would be.

"What is it, *mon amour?*" I whisper as I tug her against me and kiss the side of her head.

"Just look at that," she states as she raises a hand to motion toward the colorful sky. My gaze follows her fingers and I let myself take in what she's seeing. I pull her closer to me so her backside is pressed against my chest and I wrap my arms around her, leaning my head on her shoulder.

"It's beautiful," she says on a contented sigh, her head falling back to rest against my shoulder.

"You're beautiful," I murmur into her ear, kissing the soft skin there that drives me wild.

She shivers from my touch and slowly turns to face me. "I want to paint it."

My eyebrows lift in question. "Now?"

She shrugs almost apologetically. "Yeah, I need to at least sketch it out with a little color so I don't lose the image in my head."

Rising up on her tiptoes, Kelsie feathers a light kiss over my jaw. My hands slide down to grab her ass, fitting her snuggly against me.

How incredibly sexy would it be to watch her paint this moment? I drop my gaze to stare into her deep blue eyes.

"Can I watch you?" I ask, sounding hopeful and maybe even uncertain.

Her eyes widen like saucers. "Really? I..."

Her words trail off and she bites down on her bottom lip.

"Please? I'll be quiet and I'll stay out of your way," I add and lift a hand to tuck a loose strand of hair behind her ear.

As much as I want her naked and in my bed tonight, the idea of watching her do what she loves seems even more enticing for reasons I can't explain. Maybe it's the dreamy expression she wears when she's painting or the way her body relaxes peacefully with every brush stroke over the canvas. It's like she gets lost in a fantasy world all her own and she finds her true purpose in life.

"Okay," she agrees hesitantly, stepping back to extend her hand to me. I take it in mine as she leads the way up to the second floor landing to the attic door. When the stairs narrow, I follow behind her and I'm greeted with a perfect view of her ass. I remind myself this time is about her desires, not mine.

At least for now.

She pauses at the top of the steps and points toward the right. "You can sit on the chair over by the table."

"Okay."

Kelsie grabs a blank canvas that leans against a host of others and places it on her easel, staring at it for a long moment. I suddenly realize this is going to be harder than I thought it would be because I want nothing more than to distract her with my hands and tongue. Yet, I also don't want her to miss the opportunity to create something beautiful. Just like soccer was a lifeline for me, I feel like painting might be hers, even if she doesn't realize it.

I clear my throat. "You know what? Why don't I give you some time to get started and I'll go take a shower?"

"Oh, uh, sure," she says distractedly, as if she's already lost in her work and my voice surprised her.

I step up behind her, wrapping my arms around her waist. "Get to work, *mon amour*, because I don't know how much longer I can wait for you."

The need in my voice is already present and I slide a hungry finger down between her breasts.

"Oh," she murmurs, relaxing against my body. "Well, maybe this can wait..."

I love how quickly she responds to my touch. I want her

so much but decide for once not to listen to my dick. This is important to her, and so it's important to me.

I slide my thumb over her jawline and her eyelids flutter. "Get your thoughts on the canvas. I'll be right back up."

Hesitating only for a second at the top of the stairs, I gaze at her longingly. She's slipped on her painting overalls and already has a brush in hand.

That's my girl.

I make my way to the bathroom, taking a very quick shower because my willpower is waning. All day long my need has grown bigger and wilder. As we played the flag football game together and I watched her true happiness in the company of her friends and the way she was so uninhibited and free, it's increased my need to be close to her. To connect. To be inside her.

I hurriedly finish the shower and return to my bedroom where I throw on a pair of sweatpants and tear off a few packets of condoms from the strip.

With barely a rough dry of my hair that's sorely in need of a cut, I ditch the towel in my bathroom and head back upstairs to the attic. The quiet of the house makes me realize that our roommates are out for the evening, giving us some much needed privacy.

As Kelsie comes into view, my breath hitches.

She's so fucking beautiful. She's wearing her painting overalls with only one strap secured and has removed the shirt underneath, leaving her in just a sports bra. Her hair is pulled high up on her head in a messy bun, stray strands sticking out in different directions. Her eyes are on the canvas, but I swear her mind is a million miles away. Watching her like this in her element makes the wait to touch her so much more worth it. I'm a spectator at the sport of Kelsie's imagination coming to life, and it's awe-inspiring to see it.

God, what I wouldn't give to feel that deep passion toward something again.

I look past her at the canvas. She's begun to capture the view from this evening, complete with the bright colors in the sky reflected on the snow-capped mountaintops. And at the bottom of the landscape are two figures. They are dark, like shadows, but I know immediately who they are. *Us.* I hesitate for a second. I'm not sure if the mountains are meant to be literal or figurative. If she's painting the visual depiction of our relationship, I know we still have a long way to climb and a lot to work through. Maybe she sees that too. I still have dark secrets I haven't shared.

I'm deep in thought when Kelsie turns around to face me. She gives me a small smile and her cheeks pinken.

"It's very rough and in the early stages. I'll polish it up later with more details," she rushes to explain.

Her chest rises and falls with her quickened breaths. The light from the fixture and the one standing behind her reflects against her blonde hair, the lighter strands glinting and making her appear ethereal.

I want to tell her how beautiful she is. I want to express that she's the most gorgeous woman that I've ever seen. I want to let her know that she's never looked more perfect than at this moment.

But words fail me and I take ten steps across the room and crush her against me in a hungry kiss.

She sighs into my mouth as our kiss deepens, our tongues sliding against each other's. Her paintbrush and palette clatter to the floor and she wraps her arms around my neck. Gripping her lush ass again, I fit her against me and she wraps her legs around my waist. My cock strains inside my sweatpants in desperation to get closer.

"I need you, Kels."

She hums in response and I turn my head to scan the room for some leverage.

Walking us over to a table, I brush off some rags and paint brushes with one hand before setting her down on it. I glance down to see that my bare chest and stomach are now covered in smears of paint from her overalls.

She bites her bottom lip. "Sorry, I made a mess."

"I'm not." I pause and cup her cheek. "Never be sorry about your art. I like that it's messy." There's a splotch of yellow paint on her collarbone and I smear it up her throat before kissing her lips again.

"You're so sexy and I love watching you paint." I drop my head and lick a line up the base of her throat. "I love watching you..."

"You love watching me?" she questions as our lips touch again.

I smile against her skin. "Yeah."

Blindly fumbling with her overall strap, she giggles and helps me to unsnap it as the bib falls down to expose her bra. She raises her ass in the air and shimmies out of them. My hands roam over her tight abs, down over her belly and stop at her hip bone. I swallow.

Holy hell. She's wearing nothing on underneath. All day long she's been without panties and I didn't know it.

I suppose that's a good thing, otherwise I wouldn't have lasted long in that football game earlier.

She slips off her sports bra over her head and I step back to take her all in.

"You're the work of art, *mon amour*," I croon. I know it's cheesy as fuck, but I don't care right now. With Kelsie, I can be myself. That's one thing she's always allowed me to be. No bullshit. Just innately me.

I pull the condoms from my pocket and drop them on the table. She glances at them and then back at me.

"We don't have to use them. I haven't been with anyone else since we met in Paris, and I'm on the pill," she explains.

I lean forward and run my thumb over her lips. "Same... or at least the part about not being with anyone else," I counter with a grin.

She laughs, but it dissipates as I lick over her jawline and then down her neck.

"You have no idea how badly I want to be inside you," I whisper. I drop to my knees and spread her legs apart, pressing a kiss to her inner thigh. She's already so wet when I use my thumbs to spread her open. Then I circle her clit with my tongue and slowly sink it inside her.

Her head drops back on the table and a sexy moan escapes her lips.

"That's right, baby. Tell me how good it feels when I fuck you with my tongue," I say, remembering how much she loves dirty talk. I go back to alternating between licking her clit and sliding my tongue inside until her body begins to tremble. Her arms flail as her hands look for purchase, landing on top of my head. She fists her hands in my still damp hair.

"Oh, God! Don't stop, Hayes! I'm so close!" she yells, spurring me on as I slide two fingers inside her. I'm rewarded when she tenses against me and cries out my name. She trembles and moans as she slowly comes down off her high, her body relaxing on the table. When her hands loosen their grip from my head, I rise up to stand between her thighs, spreading her legs wider as I circle her clit with my thumb.

She reaches down and coats her fingers with her wetness and then encircles my dick, stroking me with the lubrication. I groan from the pleasure it induces.

She lines up my hard cock against her entrance, my eyes entranced with the view of the top of my crown slipping between her folds.

Then she latches her legs around me, her ankles locked around the small of my back. She prompts me forward and I slowly penetrate her walls, my length disappearing inside. I drop my head forward and release a groan at the exquisite feel of her slick heat as it surrounds me.

Our eyes lock and we're left without a single barrier between us.

I swallow at the sight of our joined bodies. "Fuck, *mon amour*. You feel so damn good." With a wicked smile, I pull out and thrust back into her. She arches off the table and cries out a moan of pleasure. I bend over and swipe my lips over her neck and jaw as I begin to pump faster and harder.

"I'm so close...I'm going to come again!" she cries out and I quicken my pace. The slapping sound our bodies make and the friction with nothing between us becomes too intense, and my balls tighten, my body rushing toward release.

I circle Kelsie's clit until I feel her tense underneath me and we both come together, my orgasm ribboning hot inside of her.

There's a moment of stillness between us and I flatten my palm to the table as our breathing evens out.

"I think I love having you watch me paint," she declares as she slowly opens her eyes.

"I think I love..." I trail off, catching myself before I say the words.

I think I still love you. I never stopped.

I clear my throat. "And I love watching you too."

I leave it at that as I pull out, reaching for a cloth on the table to wipe away the remnants of my release from her inner thighs.

The love I have for her is so great, but I'm afraid to admit it. The last thing I want to do is scare Kelsie away after we've come so far and made it here at last.

The only place I want to be.

Chapter Twenty-One

Kelsie

I stare at the canvas in front of me, angling my head from one side and then the other as I take in the symmetry, colors, and brush strokes of the image. I want to make sure I've captured every emotion I felt so that it will evoke the same from the viewer.

The idea for the painting came to me last night as I walked home hand in hand with Hayes. Spending the day with him was the best day I've ever had.

Sure, we had fun and memorable times when we were together in Paris, but the feeling that's taken hold and rooted itself in my belly recently is something entirely different.

It's a newfound intimacy and a connection that goes far beyond the attraction that I have for Hayes that began when we first met in France.

The attraction is so hot it burns in my soul and I can't get enough of him.

But now there's something else. Something deeper and

more complicated, a bond newly developed that seems to consume me.

Once the restrictions and rules were lifted and we began sharing the inner parts of ourselves, I feel closer to Hayes than I've ever been with anyone else outside of my best friends.

Hayes has somehow wormed his way inside my heart, which for so long had been guarded and kept under lock and key, and taken a piece of it. Or maybe he's given me a piece I've been missing.

Whatever it is, Hayes fuels my artistic fire like gasoline to the flames.

I take another step back to critique my work and realize there is something missing. After a few more minutes of critical self-evaluation, I decide to bring in the real artist to get her feedback.

Tugging my phone from my overalls' back pocket, I click on my aunt Desiree's contact in the messenger app. Even with the time difference between us, I figure it's a good possibility she's still awake in Paris.

The video call rings twice and then the line opens and her beautiful face appears on my screen.

"*Bonjour, ma jolie fille,*" she greets with her well-honed French accented purr. From the looks of it, she may have just returned from some sort of soiree because her hair and make-up are meticulously done and she has a bit of a slur to her words.

Champagne will do that to you.

"Hey, auntie. *Comment ça va?*"

She waves a dismissive hand in the air that's covered in bohemian-style rings and accessories, and the bangle bracelets around her wrist make a clanking sound that is a normal part of her wardrobe.

I've always loved her style. As a young girl, I thought she was some kind of beautiful princess with her flowy skirts and brightly colored clothing.

So very unlike my business-woman mother who dressed in drab, boring suits and black evening wear.

I have more love and admiration for my aunt than I do my distant and cold mom.

Desiree and I are so much alike that if the three of us were lined up, the casual observer would choose Desiree as my mother and not my own biological one.

My aunt sighs dramatically, brushing a piece of her blonde hair out of her face.

"I'm utterly exhausted, darling. I can't keep up with this new lover of mine. Jean-Phillipe is so vivacious and loves to accompany me to all the new gallery openings."

I giggle. "Vivacious, huh? Didn't you also call him a stallion in the sheets?"

Desiree leans in close and winks, giving her lips a pop. "He is all that and more, darling. God, that stud can go for hours. If only I were ten years younger."

"Puh-lease," I snort. "You have more energy than anyone I know. But I hope you're checking their ID's before you go to bed with them."

She laughs, the sound of it warm and endearing, her eyes sparkling with amusement.

My aunt has always been a happily single woman who has taught me about independence and self-reliance. She's also gone through a ton of lovers since I was old enough to understand the concept of sex. Until Hayes, I was very much following in her footsteps, both artistically and personally. I never wanted to get close to a guy because Desiree once told me that you can easily lose your identity if you lose yourself in a man.

So I took that to heart and steered clear of love and relationships.

Until I fell for Hayes. My connection with him has me rethinking all of that and it freaks me the hell out.

My aunt sits down on her oversized sofa in the same loft I stayed in when I was in Paris and throws her head back on the cushion.

"What's going on, my darling? Is something on your mind?"

I hesitate for a second, glancing up at the canvas I've been working on for hours and then I drop my gaze down at my overalls. I run a hand over my belly, the same spot where last night the paint from Hayes's chest was smeared. The intimacy of the act sends ripples of lust through my blood even now as I remember the moment.

I inhale deeply and expel the air from my lungs.

"I don't think I know how to love someone," I blurt out, the words pouring out unbidden and unexpectedly.

This gets my aunts attention, and her head snaps up, a look of confusion wrinkling her brow. "What on earth do you mean?"

I sit down cross-legged, propping my back against the wall. The floor is cold and sends a shiver up my spine.

"You know that Mom and Dad are a terrible example of what love should be."

She gives a slight nod of understanding.

My parents aren't the couple goals most people think they are. Out in public, they represent a united front for the sake of their business ventures. They do make a good team when it comes to running their successful international brand.

But the house I grew up in wasn't filled with the affection that should be part of a loving marital relationship. I'm not sure I recall a single time they hugged each other, or hugged me and Keaton, for that matter. Most of the time when they were home, they either yelled and screamed at one another or disappeared separately to their own corners of the house.

It left Keaton and me on our own much of the time and I didn't witness a good example of what love should look like. It's this nebulous concept that has eluded me for so long.

"Oh, darling, I hope you know how much I love you," she coos. "And so does your brother."

I snort. "Keaton. *Riiight.* He sure showed it poorly when he went behind my back when I wanted to go to that art camp. That proved he *doesn't* love me. He loves what my parents have to offer."

Desiree shakes her head adamantly and makes a *tsking* sound.

"No, no, no, darling. That's not true at all," she says. "I think you only have one side of the story. Have you ever spoken to your brother to ask him why he did that?"

"Hell no," I grouse, crinkling my nose at the thought of doing that. He ruined my trust. I wasn't going to ask him why he did it. "Why would I waste my time with his lies?"

"Darling, he did it out of love for you, and possibly from something I'd said to him at the time."

My heart jolts at her statement like it's been zapped by lightning.

"What do you mean? What did you say to him?"

Desiree touches her forehead, running her fingers over the hairline and sighs.

"At that time when the camp had the opening, Keaton was already in business school and he wanted both of you to follow in your parents' footsteps. But you, my darling, already possessed such a lovely artistic ability and had a passion for it. Which, of course, I loved to see and wanted to encourage."

I smile wistfully, recalling the summer when I was ten and Desiree first put a paintbrush in my hand, guiding me through the motions. Teaching me about colors and techniques. It brought me such complete and utter contentment during those hard years when I didn't feel loved.

Desiree clears her throat and lights a cigarette, taking a puff before blowing it out.

"You probably don't know this, but I struggled for over twenty years before something big happened for me. The art world is difficult, fickle, and can be devastating on your self-esteem." She inhales another drag and exhales slowly. "I may have mentioned to Keaton that maybe it would be a good thing if you attended business school so you'd have that to fall back on if art didn't work out. I guess he took that to heart and told your parents."

Something seethes inside me with red-hot anger. Disappointment curls inside my stomach And maybe even resentment toward my auntie, whom I've always loved and admired.

"How could you do that to me?" I bark out angrily. "It changed everything. I wanted to go to that camp so bad and you and Keaton ruined my chances."

I know my outburst has me sounding like an ungrateful whiny brat, but it hurts knowing my aunt may have helped sabotage my opportunities. And all this time, I've been so mad at my brother for his interference. Now I find out my aunt played a part in it too.

"Darling, it came from a place of love. You must know I only want the best for you and I didn't ever want to see you struggle the way I did. I love you like you're my own, Kelsie. And Keaton has always loved you too."

Confusion swirls inside my brain. This new revelation leaves me unsettled and unbalanced.

Desiree's next statement pushes me over the edge and has me freefalling into complete and utter chaos.

"I think it's time for you to grow up, Kelsie, and forgive your brother. Stop torturing yourself over what could have been and look at where you are and what you have now."

I let her words sink in and contemplate what it means for me.

Maybe she's right. If I'd gone to that art camp and then pursued an art school, I wouldn't be here at CFU. I wouldn't have the friends that I have.

I would never have met Hayes.

Chapter Twenty-Two

H*ayes*

It's been almost two days since I texted Holden and he has yet to respond.

The last time we spoke, he was talking animatedly about going on a road trip. It felt very much to me like he was having a manic episode because he was so fixated on it and it worried me.

Every time he behaves in this way, it's followed by a horrible depressive episode.

So, three days ago, I thought about calling my parents and telling them about it. But then I thought maybe he was just busy and that's why he hadn't responded yet. But now it's late afternoon and there's been nothing.

I feel my phone vibrate in my jeans pocket and I nearly jump out of my skin. Holding out hope it's a message from Holden, I yank it out in my hand and read the screen. Disappointment wells inside my chest when I see it's not Holden; it's a text from Killer.

> Killer: Hey, bro, you going to our training
> session early? LMK. I can give you a ride.
> It's pissing down today and figured you
> might not want to walk.

I'm still getting to know my teammates, but so far they all seem like good guys. It's a shame that the few I've become closest to will graduate this spring. Playing next fall will not be the same without Killer, Hendy, and EJ.

> Me: Yeah. That'd be great. I can meet you
> at the student union in ten.

> Killer: Cool.

I hurry across the quad, covering my head with my bag to keep from getting soaked from the downpour and meet Killer. When I open the door and slide in, he cocks his head to the side and examines me.

"Dude, you look sort of frazzled. You okay?" Killer asks me as I climb into his truck. I glance down and realize my shirt's askew and do a quick scan into the side mirror, noticing that my hair is a mess and I have bags under my eyes.

"Just worried about my brother," I admit, staring at my phone again before turning to look at Killian's profile. "I haven't heard from him in a few days. It's not like him."

Killian gives me a quick glance, turning his eyes to me before shifting them back to the road ahead. "You're close with him, huh?"

"We're twins...so..." I trail off with a shrug. But Killer's question has memories flooding my mind like a river over-flowing after a storm. Holden and I were so close before the accident. We did everything together. Hell, we even shared a best friend...until he died.

I swear I can feel Holden's pain right now and that freaks me out. It also makes me feel so goddamn guilty I could tear my hair out.

"Have you called your parents to see what they've heard?" Killer asks. "My younger brothers are always fucking around and never let my parents know where the hell they are. Maybe it's like that with yours. I wouldn't worry too much. I'm sure he's fine and just needs a little space."

I swallow nervously and shake my head. My brother has really struggled to get on with life after Kevin's death and my parents have done what they could to help him. I hate bothering them about Holden and don't want them to freak out over nothing. They've dealt with enough already as it is.

God, sometimes I wish my life was different. I wish I had never suggested we go to that party that night. I wish I hadn't been looking at my phone in the car. I wish Kevin hadn't taken his eyes off the road while driving. I wish so many things that I know can't ever come true.

"Yeah, maybe. I just have a weird feeling something's really wrong," I answer, the concern evident in my voice.

"Do you have that twin telepathy thing? Maybe that's giving you that juju. You should call them, if you're worried," he urges as he parks in front of the training facility.

He's right. I should. We pass a few players from the soccer team as we enter the building and Killer notices me watching them when he glances over at me.

"You miss it?" he asks, nodding toward a player carrying a soccer ball under his arm.

I want to say no. I want to say football was always my first choice. But I'd be lying to my new friend. I, for once, don't want to lie or pretend about how I really feel.

"Yeah. I do," I confess, glancing at him to see how he'll respond.

"You know, I used to play when I was little. So if you ever want to kick around the ball at the house, just let me know," he offers.

"Thanks, man. I'd love that," I say with a smile, but deep down the fact that I'm here playing football instead of back home playing soccer still feels like a sucker punch to my already wounded soul.

"Come on, let's go get ripped!" he says loudly as he makes a cheesy pose that has his biceps popping.

I chuckle, unable not to feel a little amused by Killer even if my mind keeps trying to pull me under the tidal wave of my guilt.

* * *

After our training session, Killer drops me off back at my house and I run inside, trying to stay dry. When I step inside the front door, I pull my phone out again and check my texts. No response.

> Me: Holden. Where are you? Please text me back or call me ASAP.

I hold my phone in my hand hoping it'll ping, but nothing happens. I set it on my bed and lie down next to it, staring absently up at the ceiling. Dread washes over me in the form of a cold sweat. My stomach knots. My heart pounds wildly. The last time I was this conflicted over Holden's state of mind was when I left Paris unexpectedly.

He's been on the brink before and I can't imagine my life without him. That's why I'm here now. I'd do anything for him, including giving up my dreams of soccer and living out his dreams of playing college football.

At least, while at CFU, I get to major in a program that interests me. I have found the perfect woman and I've met some pretty great new friends. There's also the opportunity I have to run without a limp. I grimace at that thought. Holden still walks with a cane and although he's lucky to have his leg, he'll never run again.

And it guts me.

Due to the complexities of his injuries and the almost daily therapy, Holden wasn't able to attend school on a college campus. So he tried out an online program his first year, and then the second year he was at the community college I attended, but it was never what he wanted to do. His dreams of attending a big university, playing football, going to parties, and having a serious girlfriend never came to fruition.

I punch at my mattress, hating how unfair life is.

I don't want to break his trust. I know reaching out to our parents if there's nothing wrong would destroy him and turn me into a narc.

On the other hand...if I don't, this will eat at me until I'm leveled by another panic attack. I inhale deeply, expelling the air from my lungs through the count of ten just like my therapist instructed me to do, and then another, counting backwards each time.

Finally, when I feel calm enough, I decide to call my parents as a check in and just casually ask about my brother. *Yes, that's it.*

I pick up my phone and dial my mom. She answers on the second ring sounding almost winded.

"Hayes?" she answers, her breath coming out in a rush.

"Hi, Mom," I reply, trying to figure out how to bring up

Holden without making it sound like I'm being overprotective.

She practically stammers out her reply. "*H*-how are you?"

I frown. Mom's not usually one to stumble over her words.

"Is there something wrong, Mom?" I sit up in bed and fight down the anxious, uneasy feeling that tears through my gut.

Her deep, anguished sigh tells me immediately something isn't right. My mom is always lighthearted and wears an actual smile in her voice. But right now she sounds stilted and stiff. I stand up and begin to pace, waiting for her to answer me.

"Honey, first, I just want you to know that everything is okay with Holden," she begins, and alarm bells begin blaring in my head.

"Mom...you're freaking me out! What's wrong with him?"

I stop next to my dresser and stare at a photo of my family prominently displayed on top. My throat constricts and I swallow nervously, afraid to hear the answer to my question.

"Honey, Holden was admitted to a facility today." She stops abruptly and a dead silence descends between us. Without even seeing her, I can tell she's on the verge of tears.

"Holy shit. Oh, my God. What?" My heart skips a beat. Knees buckling, I sit back down on my bed. I bend over at the waist and slam a hand through my hair, clutching the strands tightly in my grip. "Is he okay?"

Visions of him lying in a hospital bed...hooked up to machines. Nearly dead.

And then a thought hits me. Is it the medical hospital or a psych ward?

"He will be, eventually, but it will take time. Right now, your brother needs professional help. We aren't able to give him what he needs here at home. I'm so sorry." She tries to stifle a sob and my heart breaks.

It seems I'm not the only one who has held on to guilt all these years.

"Mom, you know it's not your fault. Can you tell me what happened?" I ask, fearing the truth but needing it with a desperation that claws at my soul.

"He just started ranting about the road trip and wasn't making a lot of sense." She almost chokes out the last word. "With his therapist's help, we got him to agree to check into a facility for a while. It's the best place for him." She's now crying on the other end of the line.

Goddamn, this seems hopeless.

I love my brother more than words, but sometimes I'm so damn mad at him for not making sound choices. I know that it's not his fault. I do. But I can't help getting angry at him for what he puts us through.

"I'm sorry, Hayes-bear. I'm so sorry. We should have called yesterday, but our focus was on Holden. Please forgive us."

Oh fuck.

Fuck. Fuck. Fuck.

"When did it happen?" I inquire, tears now streaming down my face.

She clears her throat. "Two nights ago."

I drop to my knees. Fuck!

Two nights ago we were texting and I said something stupid—that I missed playing soccer. This is all my fucking fault. I pushed him over the edge. I will never forgive myself.

"I'm coming home," I state emphatically, wiping away the tears that stream down my cheeks, furious with myself for not thinking about how that selfish fucking comment would affect Holden's mental state.

"No, sweetie. You don't need to just yet. Holden won't be seeing visitors for a few weeks, but I'll let him know you love him and want him to get better. Just stay there. He'd want you to stay in school," Mom pleads.

My voice breaks right along with my heart. "Mom, *please.*"

"Oh, Hayes, sweetheart. I know. I'm sorry. We'll get through this, just like we've gotten through everything else. I promise," she soothes, her voice sounding a little stronger now and more assured as if she's encouraging herself too.

"I know. I just wish I could be there with him." I press my elbows into my thighs, staring down at the floor between my feet, tears dropping to the wood one by one.

I wish I could say something to comfort her. To comfort both of us. Reminding her that Holden is strong, but right now, he's so broken. We're all broken and we will never be the same.

I just hope we can heal from it. I can deal with the scars, but the open wound from losing Kevin, and Holden's life-altering injuries, and how my life turned upside down...it all feels like too much.

"I should go. Dad will be home soon for dinner. You want him to call you later?" she asks.

"No, it's fine. I'll be fine. Please keep me updated on Holden, alright?"

"Of course, sweetie. I'll call you this weekend after we get to visit with him," she says. "And please continue to talk to your therapist, okay? It's so important to address your feelings and not bottle them up inside."

I can read between the lines. What she doesn't add is... like Holden did.

"Okay," I reply. "I'll talk to you later."

"Bye, sweetie," she says as we disconnect.

My phone trembles in my hand as I stare at it for a few minutes in a daze before my gaze darts to where my duffle bag sits in the corner of my room. I know I told her I'd stay here, but how can I? Holden needs me. He's my brother. My twin.

We've been through this together and I've been by his side up until the past six months. It was hard enough when I was away for so long in Paris, but then coming here feels so...final and life-changing. Like I'm moving on and he's stuck in place.

I'd give anything to switch places with him. He was always the one with big plans. I just figured I'd play soccer at a local college and then work for someone near our hometown. And now here I am, traveling the world, playing ball at a big university, and planning a career that could take me anywhere in the world.

Lately, I've almost become excited about the possibilities. Especially since I've been with Kelsie. She brings something alive inside me that I thought died in the accident.

I rise off the bed to my feet and falter when I reach for my bag.

Do I stay or do I go?

My gaze returns to the family photo. It was taken during happier times and it feels like a lifetime ago.

I know what I have to do, whether I want to or not.

I need to be there for Holden.

Chapter Twenty-Three

Kelsie

After much thoughtful consideration, and a few vodka and Red Bulls, I practice what I'm going to say to Keaton and finally get up the courage to call him.

Since it's completely out of the blue, and I have no idea what he's doing right now or where he is, I send him a text.

> Me: Hey, Keat...you got a second?

It takes less than 3 seconds and I see the ellipses show up. Then they disappear. Then they reappear. I stare at the blinking dots and wonder what the heck is up with him? Is he writing a thesis back in reply? Or uncertain what to say.

Finally, a text comes back with his response.

> Keaton: Ofc. Is everything okay?

I can't help but chuckle to myself over his question. Is it okay? Am I doing the right thing by reaching out and making amends? It feels like I'm finally figuring out my shit and actually adulting for once in my life.

> Me: Can I call you?

> Keaton: Oh, shit. Do I need to send bail money? Is this your one call?

I laugh at my brother's reply. He's always been funny. Serious about life, but has a sense of humor that kept me laughing all through our childhood.

I get out of the text app locating his number and hit the dial icon.

It rings once and he answers, his deep baritone voice sounding more and more like our dad's. It has a husky quality to it, but is also warm and sincere.

"Kels? Is this really you?"

"Yes, you idiot. It's me."

There's a pause and I hear him inhale a deep breath before letting it out.

"Well, for a minute there, I wasn't sure. I thought maybe aliens kidnapped you and were holding you for ransom. Otherwise, why would you call?"

He's doing what he's always done in stressful situations and that's to lighten the mood. I appreciate that about him. I kind of forgot what a good guy he is. A brother who protected me and watched out for me all those years when our parents weren't around or involved in our lives.

He has a point. I haven't called him in several years, even though he's tried many times to reach out to me. I swallow down the sorrow of knowing how stubborn I've been and the weight it's put on my heart.

"Keat, I'm calling because...well, I wanted to talk to you about..." I stop, noticing my hand shakes.

Fuck. This is much harder than I thought it would be.

I walk to my bedroom window and stare out at the newly blooming trees and plants. The snow is slowly starting to melt and spring buds have begun to pop out all around town and on campus. It gives me hope and reminds me that no matter how bleak life can be, things can regrow. People and feelings can change just like the barren winter trees that reclaim their beauty in the springtime.

"I'm sorry," I finally say in a gush of air. "I'm sorry for shutting you out of my life. For being so childish and stubborn over how I handled my anger. I see now you didn't do it to hurt me, but to help me."

Keaton sighs. "Shit, Kelsie. Do you know how bad I've felt all this time knowing I broke your trust in me? It killed me that it ruined our relationship."

"I know," I whisper, feeling tears suddenly well up in my eyes. "I'm sorry I was such a bratty, stubborn sister. I guess you could chalk it up to being young and stupid, not understanding the world the way you do."

"Yeah, sometimes I wish I didn't." He scoffs sharply. I can almost see him run a hand through his perfectly-kept blond hair. I used to tease him because he never had a strand out of place. "The world is fucking hard, Kels. Trust me."

His response piques my curiosity. It's not something I'd ever expect to hear from my normally optimistic brother.

I take a seat at my desk and set the phone in my desk cradle, placing it on speaker. Then I grab my make-up bag, pulling out some concealer and tools.

"Everything okay with work?"

Although we haven't spoken, I know Keaton graduated and immediately took a very prominent position in my parents' company as Assistant VP of Operations. A role not many people just out of college would ever get.

I can hear Keaton as he sucks his teeth, a habit he's always had, indicating his stress.

"Between you and me, working with your parents is not an easy task," he says honestly.

I bite my lip to keep from saying *I told you so* and keep quiet.

"I've been trying to help them move into a new online ordering platform and they refuse to listen. They say it costs too much money, even though I've shown them the return on investment it will give us."

"They've never listened to us. Why would it change now?" I state with a short laugh.

"True. I guess I had these grand delusions that since they wanted me to join the business so badly, they'd actually allow me to offer up suggestions for improvements."

I add some rosy tint to my cheeks and lips, brushing the color with a few strokes of my fingertip, contemplating the idea of me working for my parents someday. If my brother, who is very diplomatic, has trouble with them, how in the world would I get along with my wiseass mouth?

Keaton laughs softly. "Sorry, I shouldn't be complaining to you about this. That's not why you called. But I'm really glad you did, Kelsie, and I'd love to see you soon. Maybe we can go somewhere this summer after your semester ends? Do you have plans yet?"

A strange feeling flutters and then knots inside my belly. I drop my hand to my stomach and hold it there, trying to make sense of the anxiety that grows when I think about not being with Hayes this summer. We haven't talked about what we're doing or if he'll be going home to Colorado. I'm sure he will since he wants to see his family.

My voice comes out in a croak. "I don't know yet. I'd love to go back to Paris for a month to see DD. Otherwise, I have no plans. But maybe you can come visit over spring break in a few weeks if you have time? We usually go to a friend's cabin for skiing."

"That sounds fun. Let me look at my schedule and I'll let you know."

"Cool. I'd really like to see you too, Keat."

"Love ya, sis. Later, alligator."

"After awhile, crocodile."

We end the call and I stare up into the mirror and realize I'm smiling. And the first person I want to tell about the end of my estrangement with my brother is Hayes.

Dabbing a bit more color to my lips, I give them a satisfying smack before I rush out my bedroom and take the stairs two at a time. I can't wait to tell Hayes about my call with Keaton. And to finally bare my soul to Hayes and tell him that I'm in love with him and want to make plans to continue what we have together.

I want to be with him this summer. I'm not sure what that involves, but I'm willing to do or go wherever he wants.

Hayes's door is slightly ajar and I give it a knock and walk in.

"Hey, lover," I start to say and then get a good look around his room. It's a mess. Like a tornado destroyed it. There are clothes and books strewn everywhere and Hayes is standing at his bed with his back to me. He appears to be packing a bag.

"What are you doing?"

The moment he swings his head over his shoulder and I see the dark expression in his eyes, I know it's not good. I begin to walk toward him.

"I'm leaving."

My steps falter. "Leaving? Where are you going?"

Hayes continues to throw things in a bag, ignoring me when I come up to stand beside him. "Colorado."

"What? When?"

He snorts like this is obvious and I'm just slow. "Now."

I take a small step backward and survey the surroundings, trying to figure out what's happening right now.

Everything was fine with Hayes earlier this morning when he left my bed and went to his workout and practice. We'd planned on getting together tonight to finalize our project that we need to present in class next week. To say this has taken me completely off-guard is an understatement.

"Why? And how are you going to get there?"

Hayes's words are clipped and sharp. He swings around to me and his eyes blaze with an emotion I've never seen him express before.

"Jesus Christ, Kelsie. Is this the Spanish Inquisition? Do I need to tell you everything that I do?"

His words are cold and harsh and slash my gut like a machete.

I swallow down the tears that prick behind my eyes. "Well, no, but obviously something's going on. I'll help if you let me."

I use this opportunity to slowly move behind him and place my hands on his shoulders that tense under my grip.

Hayes stops his frantic packing and then spins around on me, shrugging my hands from his body. His brows narrow and his nostrils flare.

"Oh, really? You can help get my brother out of the psych facility that I put him in?"

More questions pop inside my head, swirling like a

school of fish in the ocean, moving fluidly from one direction to another. Why? When? How?

Instead of asking, I tackle Hayes in a bear hug and hold him close.

"I'm sorry, baby. Whatever happened, it's not your fault."

For a moment, Hayes remains still in my embrace, his arms hanging limply at his sides. As if he's holding on by a single thread and he wants to let it go. I nestle my face into the crook of his neck and breathe in his scent that is all too familiar to me now.

And then he jerks away. "You're wrong, Kels. It *is* my fault. And I have to go home to fix it for my brother right this minute. He can't wait any longer."

He snatches up his bag from the bed, ready to walk out the door as he throws it over his shoulder.

Hoping to keep him from making an impetuous mistake, I grab his wrist, holding him in place.

My voice is soft, almost a whisper. "Whatever you did for Holden, I know you did out of love, Hayes. I understand that now."

He doesn't look at me, but I step in closer, holding on to his hand, slipping my fingers through his. "I talked to Keaton today and I finally forgave him. I know Holden will forgive you too."

"He will never forgive me, Kels. And our situations are nowhere near the same."

He extracts his hand from mine but doesn't leave. When he finally turns to glance down at me, a strand of his dark hair covers his eyes and his cheek. I lift my hand to brush it away and he flinches.

"You not going to a prestigious art camp is nothing like my brother's time in a psych ward."

Now it's my turn to flinch. I gasp at this revelation and my heart drops to my toes.

"I ratted him out and now look where he's at," he grumbles with a shake of his head, voice gruff with emotion. "I put him there. And I need to get him out."

I try one last time to reason with him.

"Hayes, baby...have you considered that maybe this is for the best? That whatever you think you did to him was the turning point that will get him the help he needs?"

He makes another disgruntled noise. "You have no idea what you're talking about because you don't know him. So just stay out of my life and let me go. Okay?"

He stomps toward the stairs, stopping just at the top of the landing while I remain frozen in place in the middle of his room.

All I see from here is his profile. He doesn't even look my way.

He doesn't even care that he's leaving me again.

"Goodbye, Kels."

I blink past the tears and watch him disappear down the stairs.

At least—this time—he said goodbye in person.

Chapter Twenty-Four

Hayes

My mind is in rapid fire mode as I walk quickly toward the bus station on the other side of campus at the town center. A movie reel of memories cycles through my head on fast-forward.

Kevin and I laughing together at the party the night of the accident.

Holden, in critical condition, lying in the hospital bed.

My reluctant, but necessary decision to play football.

Going to Paris.

The first time I saw Kelsie.

The fear that consumed me the entire flight back from Paris.

Unexpectedly seeing Kelsie again.

I give my head a quick shake, trying to clear it as angry tears threaten to spill from my eyes. I wipe them away with the back of my hand and walk faster down the side streets toward town.

I inhale a deep, cleansing breath, but instead of feeling better, it makes me feel worse. I have a thousand excuses why I didn't think Holden should go out alone on that road trip and he didn't deserve the outcome of my call to our parents. I should have just asked him to wait until my spring break and offered to go on the trip with him.

It's my fault my parents sent him to the psych facility. I shouldn't have been so harsh with my text messages.

Fuck. I can't get anything right.

I stare down the block as the busy bus station comes into view. It's behind the train depot at the end of Main Street and there is a row of benches outside along the brick wall. Taking a seat to wait, I scan the area in search of something...searching for what, I don't know.

I drop my bag to the ground in front of my feet and stare down at it, examining the lumpy, dark canvas material like it holds all the answers to this terrible situation.

The bag belongs to Holden. I grabbed his by mistake when I packed for school in a hurry after returning home from Paris. It had been a whirlwind of chaos before I had to get myself out here to CFU for the new semester.

Holden's name is visible on the tag, written in his perfect handwriting. He always had nicer handwriting than I did. He was always better at everything. I take another deep breath. In and out.

I feel out of control. *Everything* feels out of control.

The only thing that grounded me is the woman I just walked away from. Again. The woman I still love and can't stop loving, but now I've ruined the second chance I was given with her. I'll never get another one. Kelsie will never forgive me.

"Fuck!" I spit out harshly, the unexpected noise surprising an older lady who suddenly appears in front of me on one of those motorized scooters. She makes a small noise of disapproval.

We catch eyes and I mutter my apology. "Sorry."

I drop my head in my hands, threading my fingers through my hair that curtains around my face. I want to pull it all out, mired in this hopeless feeling.

"Are you all right, my dear?" the lady asks, tentatively approaching me.

I shake my head, not bothering to look up.

She directs her scooter next to me at the end of the bench. "You don't look okay" she says blatantly with zero tact.

Thanks a lot, lady.

"Why don't you tell an old lady your problems? I've got nothing left but time," she offers kindly.

I slowly raise my head, swiveling my neck to face her. She must be in her eighties with white hair, a pair of wrinkled hands that grasp the handle bars, a bag with bread sticking out from the top in the front basket.

"I'm Ruth," she says by way of introduction, taking one of those hands and holding it out to me.

I accept it, shaking it gently. "Hayes."

"Hayes. That's a nice name for such a troubled young man. Are you going somewhere? Are you a student at CFU?" she asks. "My grandson attends CFU."

I nod. "In answer to your questions, yes."

"Well, Hayes, tell me your story. I'm a very good listener and I'd love it if you'd share it with me," she says, brooking no argument, as she folds her hands in her lap.

I don't know why, but I tell her everything, and I mean *everything*. From the night of the party with Kevin and Holden, all the way up to today. We sit there for at least an hour and when I finish, I look into Ruth's wise eyes. I expect to see pity, but instead she wears an expression I can't quite read.

"I'm a horrible person, aren't I?" I finally state, breaking the silence between us, knowing she must think I'm awful. Because I certainly do.

"Oh, honey, you aren't horrible. You're human. And I think that girl, what'd you say her name is?" Ruth asks with a wave of her hand.

"Kelsie."

"Yes, Kelsie. I think you'll be making one of the biggest mistakes of your life, one you'll regret forever, if you don't go back and tell that girl what she means to you."

I contemplate this for a moment, remembering the heartbroken expression on Kelsie's face when I left.

"I know you may be right, but Holden needs me. I need to fix that first," I explain adamantly. I'm not sure if it's to get her on board with my plan or to reassure myself.

She shakes her head and then extends a shaky hand to grip my forearm. "I know it's a tough love thing to do, but he's not in the proper frame of mind right now. Only time will heal him. Then he will hopefully see you did it from the heart. But right now, he won't be able to hear you over the pain he's in."

My chest squeezes with a sharp stab of regret knowing how much pain he must have endured and suffered these past three years.

Ruth continues. "The silver lining is that he's still a young man and has plenty of time for road trips and other things once he's better. Let him work on himself without you for a minute. He needs time to heal and deal with that grief on his own, just like you do."

Wow, I've never thought of it that way. This woman is wise and perceptive.

"Thank you, Ruth. You're very good at doling out advice. Were you a therapist at some point?" I ask, curious because she seems to have such wisdom about my situation.

Ruth laughs lightly, a small rasp to her voice, and clucks her tongue. "Oh, no...I've just lived a life well-versed in grief, love, and regret. Thankfully, with time, it heals. And your pain will too."

"I hope so," I add, feeling hopeful for the first time in a long time.

Leaning closer, she presses her bony shoulder against mine, her eyes staring at me intently. "But don't wait, Hayes. If she's the one, then tell her everything. Women need to know what's in your head and in your heart. Don't lose Kelsie because you are too afraid to talk about your pain."

"What if it's too late?" I whisper as I feel those tears welling again, hating myself for being so vulnerable in front of this woman I just met.

Ruth turns her torso toward me, extending her arms to hug me. I bury my face against her shoulder as she pats my back and lets me cry it out.

"Kelsie reached out to Keaton, right? There's always hope, right?" she points out as she strokes my back.

I nod a little. She's not wrong. Pulling back, I wipe my tears and look into her kind eyes.

"Thanks, Ruth," I whisper.

She smiles and gives my cheek a little pat. "You're welcome, Hayes."

Then she motions to a house down the street. "I live over there in that blue one. You can stop by any time. And maybe you can come over with my grandson, Emmett Hudson."

I manage a laugh. "Really? EJ's one of my teammates."

"Well, isn't that a lucky coincidence." She motions for me to get up. "Now go on! Go get that girl."

I grab my bag and stand, tossing it over my shoulder before offering Ruth my hand to shake.

"Thanks again, Ruth. I'll definitely stop by sometime."

"Good, good. I want to know what happens. You take care, my dear."

Giving her a wave goodbye, I rush back to the house, going from a quick walk to a jog in hopes with every step that I haven't completely fucked things up with Kelsie and she'll be willing to forgive me.

When I reach the door, I pause and swallow nervously before opening it. I see Eleanor in the living room with her headphones on and Parker is in the kitchen, but no Kelsie.

I head down the hallway to her bedroom where the door is shut, calling out her name. "Kelsie! Are you in there?"

Opening the door, I find an empty room and no Kelsie. I spin back around on my heels and out to the kitchen.

"Hey, Parker, have you seen Kelsie?"

She lifts her head and turns to look at me over her shoulder.

"Yeah, she said she was going to some ceremony at the Center for the Arts." She shrugs, taking a bite of something from her plate. "Don't know what it is, but she was all dressed up."

"Thanks," I say, waving a hand and taking off in a sprint out of the house again.

I try to come up with an answer why she'd be attending some ceremony at the arts building and then it dawns on me.

It's the art contest I mentioned to her and pleaded with her to submit the painting she'd been working on of the two of us.

The last I knew, though, she said she wasn't interested in sharing a piece of her heart with the public.

But maybe...just maybe she ended up doing just that.

I stop at the end of the walkway and shoot off a couple of texts, but don't wait for the reply as I make my way to campus to find the arts building.

In the event she's there, I can finally tell her everything. I'll put it all out on the line—the good, the bad, the ugly, and the godawful truth—and if she'll still have me and wants to be with me like I do her, then we can move on.

Because I've learned a lot about myself this semester.

I might wear the scars from the accident forever, but that's all they'll be...scars. Little reminders of who I am and the experiences I've had.

I'm not the boy who caused an accident. Or the boy who lost his friend. Or the man who can't help his brother or the football player who never dreamed of playing the game.

I am a man who can forgive himself for things that were out of his control and move on to live a life that has meaning and purpose.

And right now, my purpose is to find the woman I love and tell her everything.

To tell her she is my everything.

Chapter Twenty-Five

Kelsie

I have no time to waste staying at home and crying any more tears over Hayes' departure. He's made his decision to leave, which means he's made his decision about us. I'm not important enough for him to stay.

I'm also running late. The contest unveiling event and presentation ceremony at the Center for the Arts starts at three.

Today they announce the winners in each category. I'd barely finished my piece in time to submit it for judging and even then, I wasn't sure if I wanted to enter.

Although Hayes had encouraged me—even begged me —to submit it last week, it wasn't until after I spoke with my aunt and considered all that transpired to lead me up to meeting Hayes that I finally bit the bullet and dropped it off, along with my submission form, to the arts office.

I didn't tell anyone about my decision. Not Grace, not Lucy. Not even Hayes, even though it was his idea. I hid the truth from him because it made me feel vulnerable to be so exposed and have everyone see the truth in my art: *I'm in love.*

But it doesn't matter now. My art will be on display, along with my love life, in a public forum and I couldn't tell Hayes even if I wanted to because, for all I know, he's already on his way back to Colorado.

I finish my hair and make-up and then look at the time once again that's listed on the flyer before setting it back down on my desk. The event begins in twenty minutes.

I pack up my bag, adjust the strap of my bra underneath my shirt, and walk out the door with a straight spine and confident smile on my face.

It feels good to do this on my own.

It reminds me that I don't ever need anyone but myself to do what I want. I'm self-assured and independent. This thing with Hayes, although wonderful at times, has taken me on a roller coaster of emotion. The ups and downs since meeting him had twisted me up in a bundle of knots. Being on my own again will feel better.

I tell myself this several times like a mantra as I walk at a quick pace through the quad and enter the arts building.

The room is packed with students and faculty, a loud din of chatter filtering through the crowd. A guy dressed in a suit coat stands at the entryway and hands me a pamphlet.

"Thanks," I say, accepting the handout and scanning the seats to find a spot.

I take a seat next to a girl I know in the rows reserved for contest entrants. From the looks of it, there are two full rows and about twenty-five students.

"Hey, Kelsie. Are you as nervous as I am?" the girl, Nadia, asks in a tittering voice, an anxious smile on her face.

I shrug noncommittally. "I don't know. I guess. Now that I see how many people entered, maybe I am a little nervous."

Nadia flaps a hand and makes a scoffing sound. "Oh, please. I'm sure yours is fantastic. Which category did you enter?"

I cast my gaze down to the pamphlet and see the categories listed and the names of each student and their submission titles.

"Oh, mine is impressionism."

She sighs. "Ooh, I just love that style. Mine is contemporary. But I'm most interested in seeing all the graffiti art. It's so cool what these artists can come up with."

I nod in agreement out of politeness, not really interested in that style myself. Nadia continues to chatter nervously until the lights on the stage go up and the curtain opens. The head of the art department, Sophia Hernandez, walks out on stage to applause.

"Thank you all for joining us this afternoon for a remarkable show of talent and unique artistic views from our student artists," she begins with another round of applause from the audience. "At CFU, we pride ourselves on encouraging development among our youth of today in hopes they will continue to strive and flourish, producing art that will benefit our world and future."

As Sophia is speaking, I feel my phone vibrate in my bag. I'd silenced it before I came in the room to avoid being interrupted or impolite. For a minute, I consider ignoring it but bend over and extract the device. I stare down at the message.

Hayes: Where are you?

Hayes: I need to talk to you.

Hayes: Please, Kels. I have to tell you everything.

Hayes: I'm coming to find you.

I wrinkle my nose in confusion. Does this mean he's back on campus? And he didn't leave after all? Something in my belly flutters. My heart races with anticipation.

I'm about to text back when Nadia elbows me in the arm. My head snaps up to her.

"This is your category," she whispers. "She's going to announce the winner."

Excitement surges through my bloodstream but I don't know if it's because of the announcement or the sheer shock from learning that Hayes didn't leave like he said. Hayes is here and he's looking for me.

"And this year's winner of the impressionism style category is..." she pauses for dramatic effect and I feel my heart skip a beat. "*Mon Amour* by junior student, Kelsie Dannon."

Nadia screams in delight and grabs my shoulders, shaking me like I'm a birthday present she's going to unwrap. I jolt in my chair, struggling to comprehend what I think I heard. Did my name just get called?

I stare wide-eyed up at the front of the stage, glued to my seat until Nadia nudges me to get to my feet. The sound of applause and cheering is muffled by the noise inside my head.

Sophia smiles broadly as I walk up the steps toward her. She extends her hand to shake mine and presents me with a certificate of achievement, along with a cash prize of $250.

"Congratulations, Kelsie," Sophia says into the mic on the podium. "Would you like to say a few words and tell us what the painting represents to you? What would you like the viewers to feel when they look at our artwork?"

I accept the award, holding on tightly as I stare out at the audience. It's a sea of people, but somehow my gaze manages to land on the boy I fell in love with in Paris over six months ago.

Hayes is standing in the back of the room, his dark eyes are warm and filled with pride.

I smile as I lean down to speak into the mic. "It represents first love. Heartbreak. And second chances."

When I step back, there's more applause and I turn to leave the stage, heading straight back toward Hayes, who has his arms flung wide open.

I throw my arms around his back and clutch him tight as he embraces me in his strong hold.

"I'm so fucking proud of you, baby. But, fuck, I'm so sorry for leaving you again like I did," he whispers, kissing the top of my head. I feel tears stream down my face as I press my cheek against his chest. We cling to one another as if we're each a life raft in the middle of the ocean.

"Why did you leave me again? If you love me, you'd stay."

How ironic that I always thought that about my parents, who would so often be gone; I felt their absence was because they didn't love me.

Hayes pulls back enough to gaze down into my face. "There are things I haven't told you about. I haven't been completely honest with you. Can we go somewhere more private?"

I glance around and see the exit, grabbing his hand and tugging him out the door and down the hall to an open room.

He closes the door behind him and I hit the light switch before turning around to face him.

"What things haven't you told me?"

"The night of the accident..." he pauses, swallowing as if mustering the courage to continue. "When Kevin was driving, I held my phone up to show him something. That's how the accident happened. Maybe he had a drink or two, but it wasn't because he was drunk. He swerved and lost control because he took his eyes off the road and then over-corrected when he veered too hard. The accident was all my fault," he explains, his voice choked up and full of emotion.

"Oh, Hayes. Baby," I respond, cupping his face in my palms. Tears stream down his cheeks and I lean up and kiss them away, tasting the salty wetness of his grief.

"I didn't want to tell you because...I didn't want you to be disappointed in me. I just wanted someone to think I'm not a terrible person," he admits.

"Hayes, you could never be a terrible person," I argue, my gaze searching his, pleading my case. "You're so good. You're good to me and to those you love."

He pulls me back into his arms and holds me tight. "I don't know about that. But I do know that you're the most important person to me and I'm so sorry that I pushed you away. Self-loathing has been eating me away for years. I tried to bury it, but it broke free when I found out what happened to Holden. I felt like I failed him again and, in turn, failed you too."

"I'm not going to lie, when you left, it hurt." I grab his hand and bring it to my heart, holding it there he can feel it beating. "But you didn't fail me. You came back, you're here now, and that's all that matters."

"I'm here now, and I'm never letting you go again, *mon amour*," he murmurs against my hair. He pulls back and cups my face in his hands, staring down at me in amazement. "Oh, my God, Kelsie. Your painting won! I'm so proud of you."

His mouth crashes into mine, capturing me in a thorough kiss.

When our mouths separate, I smile up at him. "Thanks for being my muse."

"Kels, I want to be your muse for as long as you want me. I'll be the best muse, boyfriend, lover you'll ever have."

I snuggle into him, nestling my face in his chest.

"I guess it's true what they say," I murmur quietly and reverently. "Love really does bring out the best in people."

Epilogue

Hayes - Fall Semester

The lights of the stadium come into focus, shining bright over the field at the end of the tunnel.

It's the first home game of the season and my teammates surround me, each of us amped, jumping on our feet with adrenaline pumping through our veins. For the first time ever, I'm excited to play football. Not for Holden this time, but for me. CFU has become my home away from home and Kelsie is a big part of that.

The crowd roars loudly as we begin to take the field in a sea of red and white. The noise is deafening and it makes me feel alive and full of possibilities.

It's still a bit unnerving to feel this way, completely opposite to the heaviness that once sat on my shoulders and has since been lifted away.

The team makes our way to the bench where some of us sit, listening to the announcer as he does his thing. But all the surrounding noise dies away as I search for and find

Kelsie in the crowd. She's waving a giant red sign with black lettering that reads, "#17 on the field, #1 in my heart."

Keaton, her brother, sits next to her, clapping and laughing as she bobs up and down, waving her sign like a lunatic. Over the spring and summer, I've gotten to know Keaton a little bit and find him to be a good guy. I'm glad he and Kelsie have worked through their issues, just as Holden and I have too.

My gaze lands on Holden, sitting a row behind Kelsie with my former football teammates who all graduated last spring. When I stare up at his face, Holden wears a smile I never thought I'd see him give so freely.

Killer is saying something that has all of them—Grace, EJ, Lucy, and even Hendy—laughing hysterically. It fills my heart to full knowing that Holden got through the dark times and came out with a new perspective on his life.

The opposing team won the coin toss, so I get up and head to the sideline area to warm up. I'll be taking the field at any given point.

Even Hendy is here today. He didn't graduate in the spring like the other players and decided not to go pro, after all. Instead, he's finishing his degree and even though he's no longer eligible to play, he's still got football in his blood and is here cheering alongside everyone else.

It's a quick 4th down for the Stallions and our offensive line takes the field, where our new quarterback, Colson Levitt, makes an amazing play, throwing a perfect spiral to Andre Johnson, a wide receiver. Andre somehow manages to bolt down the field, dodging a few attempted tackles. My teammates and I cheer as he dashes into the end zone and scores a touchdown.

"Get out there, Mac!" Coach prompts me as I pick up

my helmet and slip it on over my head. I run out onto the field, taking my spot to line up the kick to get my team that additional point.

The sound of the crowd chanting my name gives me another surge of adrenaline, the noise spurring me on and dousing my nerves with a steely calm. I wait for the ball to be snapped and with one fluid motion, I kick it with the precision I've been practicing all my life. The noise of the stadium dulls as everyone watches the ball sail perfectly between the uprights. Another thunderous collective roar from the stadium and my teammates congratulate me with claps on the back as I rush off to the sideline.

There's not much better than this feeling right now. It's like being on top of the world.

Speaking of top of the world, I glance back up at the stands and see my girl's eyes on me. She's screaming my name and I squint to read the new sign she turns around and I laugh. It says: "Go #17! My boyfriend kicks balls!"

That's right, *mon amour*, I'm *your* motherfucking boyfriend.

Kelsie spins around and exchanges hugs with Holden and our friends. It's hard to believe we're here in this place after so many difficulties and setbacks.

Holden has continued to go to weekly therapy sessions and just recently enrolled back in school to begin classes in cybersecurity at the community college at home. He's still living with my parents and he's still working on physical therapy for his leg, but he's gotten stronger and now even walks without a cane, something doctors weren't sure he'd ever do again.

He started new meds for his depression and he's doing some group therapy with accident survivors too. I am so fucking proud of him. My heart splits open wide at the joy I feel knowing he's come so far in his healing process.

His progress has been a huge help to me. The boulder I once carried started to lift as he began to improve. I hadn't realized how much of his pain I consumed on top of my own.

And then there's my Kelsie. I look up at her again and our eyes meet. She grins down at me with a wave and I nod my chin and arch my brows.

"Bro, she's got you by the balls," Andre says as he takes a seat next to me. I elbow him in the ribs.

"Fuck off, Dre. She can have my balls. She can have all of me and I don't even care," I mutter.

He laughs. "You are pussy-whipped."

"Fuck yeah, I am," I agree. "When you have a girl like that, there's no other way to be."

I turn back to Kelsie.

"*I love you*," she mouths, her full lips turning up into a sexy smile and she gives me the heart shape with her hands.

I return the sentiment.

All of a sudden, I hear the crowd roar and lots of *oohs* and a*wws*. Dre punches my arm and I look over to see my face being projected on the jumbotron at the end of the field.

My teammates all make hearts with their hands and kissy noises, calling out, "I love you, pookie bear" and "I love you more, babycakes."

I roll my eyes and laugh. I don't even care if they make fun of me. The whole world might as well know that Kelsie is mine and I'm hers. Fuck 'em. As long as we have each other, it doesn't matter.

I look back up at Kelsie and she holds yet another new sign in her grasp. I grin when I read it.

"#17 is MY football player."

"Damn, right, *mon amour!* Damn right!" I yell.

And as I stare up at the woman I love, I know I've found my person. I might be her football player, but she's my everything.

THE END

Acknowledgments

Sierra Hill would like to thank:

My friend and dancing queen, Apryl, who gleefully provided me with the first line of this book last fall - newly single and excited for what came next. Apryl, may you find your HEA and if you must, kiss a lot of hot guys in the meantime!

A HUGE thanks from both Sierra and Sarah go out to Rachel @rrbookreviews who has been immensely helpful to us in proofing this book and showing great support and love for our books. You're awesome, Rachel!

S.E. Rose would like to thank:

Mr. Rose for giving us a crash course on all the finer points of college football transfers. Who knew there were so many rules?

To Dani Sanchez for your help in acquiring the audiobook deal for this series. We can't wait to hear our books come to life!

And to all our ARC team readers - we can't thank you enough for the time you spend reading, reviewing and giving us feedback. You are why we do this!

About the Authors

USA Today & International Bestselling romance author, **S.E. Rose** lives near Washington D.C. with her family.

When she's not wrangling her cats or keeping up with her kids, she's plotting her next story.

She loves all things wine, coffee, and cats.

In her non-existent free time, she enjoys traveling, going to concerts, binging on her favorite shows, and reading, especially if it's a good mystery or comedy.

Learn more about upcoming books from S.E. Rose at www.seroseauthor.com or follow her on Facebook, Twitter, and Instagram.

Sierra Hill is a ***RONE Award-Winning*** author of ***Game Changer***, as well as over 40 novels, including the college sports series, ***Courting Love***, and her newest hockey series, ***Vancouver Vikings***.

Subscribe to her email list and download a FREE book here: https://www.sierrahillbooks.com//newsletter

Also by S.E. Rose and Sierra Hill

College football - CFU Series

Falling for the Fake Boyfriend (Lucy and Emmett)

Falling for the Roommate (Grace and Killian)

Falling for the Football Player (Kelsie and Hayes)

Falling for the Quarterback (Hendy and Lottie)

**Looking for some steamy small
Town/firefighter/Brothers action?**

Check out our co-written Fanning the Flames series

Burned

Ignited

Scorched